Praise for Maria Grace

"Grace has quickly become one of my favorite authors of Austen-inspired fiction. Her love of Austen's characters and the Regency era shine through in all of her novels." **Diary of an Eccentric**

"Maria Grace is stunning and emotional, and readers will be blown away by the uniqueness of her plot and characterization" **Savvy Wit and Verse**

"Maria Grace has once again brought to her readers a delightful, entertaining and sweetly romantic story while using Austen's characters as a launching point for the tale." **Calico Critic**

I believe that this is what Maria Grace does best, blend old and new together to create a story that has the framework of Austen and her characters, but contains enough new and exciting content to keep me turning the pages. ... Grace's style is not to be missed.. **From the desk of Kimberly Denny-Ryder**

A Spot of Sweet Tea

Hopes & Beginnings

Maria Grace

White Soup Press

Published by: White Soup Press

A Spot of Sweet Tea: Hopes and Beginnings
Copyright © 2015 Maria Grace

The characters and events portrayed in this book are ficti-
tious or are used fictitiously. Any similarity to actual
persons, living or dead, events or locales is entirely coinci-
dental and not intended by the author.

For information, address
author.MariaGrace@gmail.com

ISBN-10: 0692530975
ISBN-13: 978-0692530979 (White Soup Press)

Author's Website: RandomBitsofFaascination.com
Email address: Author.MariaGrace@gmail.com

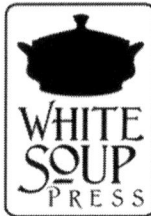

Dedication

For my husband and sons.
You have always believed in me.

Table of Contents

Four Days

IN April

April 9, 1812

DARCY STALKED FROM the parsonage in such haste the housekeeper barely opened the front door in time. The spleen of that woman! The unmitigated impertinence! She painted him a villain … a vulgar villain!

He mounted his horse and turned away from Rosings. He needed quiet and space to think. Neither were possible in the vicinity of Lady Catherine de Bourgh.

… you are the last man in the world I could be prevailed upon to marry …

His hands quivered and his whole body trembled. The sketch she had drawn of his character! In her eyes, he was no better than…than Wickham! Had anyone ever considered him so low?

Preposterous, utterly and completely preposterous!

Aunt Catherine might believe herself celebrated for her character, but that was her way of assuring herself of her own superiority. Ask any man in Derbyshire, and he would vouch for the Darcy name. Every tenant and farmer and servant on Pemberley would bear witness to him as a fair and generous master who cared more for his people than they had right to expect. He had no desire to be anything less than that.

Yes, that sharp-tongued slip of a woman would impugn the Darcy name? This was not to be borne.

He urged his horse to a trot. The pounding rhythm of its hooves commanded his attention as he matched his movements to his mount's. The country side blurred around him, and he gave into the moving meditation of the ride. The angst, the anger, the raw burning in his soul yielded to the cadence filling his being, and faded to a dull emptiness that no longer threatened to overwhelm him.

Would that he might spend the rest of the day in such escape, but neither he, nor the horse, had the strength to continue indefinitely. He settled the beast back to a walk, and the fragile peace he had found ebbed away.

Neither speed nor distance had changed the specter that hung over his head. She was out there in the world, thinking very ill of him indeed.

That he could not bear. His pride, his character … and his wounded sensibilities could not leave it lie. She may have refused his offer, but she would have his defense.

But how? Surely she would not entertain his company again.

He guided his horse to a tree-lined path, deep with shade. The cool air chilled the sweat on his face and neck cold as her words.

… had you behaved in a more gentleman-like manner …

Gentleman-like? Gentleman-like? Never in all his days had his manners been so censured!

He was a gentleman, by his station, by his breeding. Everything about him screamed so.

Everything but her.

On what point had he been mistaken? Had she any dower to bring to Pemberley? Were her connections so desirable? Were any of her family—save her and her elder sister—not an affront to society? Of course he disliked the prospect. Why should he not? Indeed who in his position would do different?

Bingley did not seem to mind.

Darcy wiped sweat from his brow with the back of his hand.

But Bingley's situation was different. Very different. Entirely different. How could they even bear comparison? He was not even a gentleman, not yet.

But no one ever considered him ungentlemanly. Bingley was universally regarded wherever he went.

How would he have offered marriage to a Miss Bennet?

Doubtless he would have flattered her vanity—told her of her beauty, of her fine eyes and charming wit.

The corner of Darcy's lips turned up. Her eyes were astonishing. How long had it been since he thought her only tolerable enough?

Bingley would have never stopped there. He would have waxed on about his tender feelings and how he would treasure her all the days of his life.

Pretty words and noble sentiments, but none of which were things he would ever have thought to say.

No…he would never share Bingley's faculty with words.

But perhaps he might not have voiced his internal struggles over his own, will reason and character so loudly. Was it not imperative to be truthful in such matters, though?

He raked his hair and settled his hat back into place.

Fitzwilliam, just because something is true does not mean it needs to be spoken.

How often had his mother reminded him?

It is difficult for people to hear such things and not believe you intend to injure them with your words, even when to you it is a simple statement of fact. A gentleman must know when to keep some facts to himself.

His horse paused to take a mouthful of weeds growing beside the road. Darcy patted its neck. Perhaps his mother and Miss Elizabeth were correct; offering those truths in the midst of an offer of marriage was ungentlemanly.

Now what?

How could he correct her views, convince her he was not the unprincipled lout she currently believed? Talking to her was out of the question—she would never admit him.

Fitzwilliam? No—he shuddered—best he never know of this humiliating debacle. No one must know.

Then how?

A letter, it was the only alternative. But a lady did not receive letters from a man not her betrothed. A gentleman did not write them. A lady would not read one.

She already thought him ungentlemanly, so there was little lost there. Her intelligence—and curiosity—might certainly induce her to read such a missive.

What choice did he have? She would never marry him, but at least she might not regard him so irredeemable, after all.

He turned his horse toward Rosings. He had a very long letter to write.

April 10, 1812

ELIZABETH SET OUT early lest she encounter Mr. Collins in the house. The wounds were too fresh, the shock still too vivid to remain concealed. Though he was by no means an observant man, even he would see it all on her face.

She must settle herself in the quiet morning mists, among the green and growing things, where things were as they seemed, and she might trust her own discernment. Perhaps then, just perhaps, she might appear in company again.

She turned down the lane, away from Rosings. She dare not venture near the gates nor look into the park. How could she ever enter Rosings again, knowing *he* might be found there?

The spleen, the audacity! Had a more insulting, more humiliating offer of marriage ever made? He could have invited her to come under his protection with far less affront to her sensibilities.

But no—against his will, against his reason, against even his very character he made her an offer. Her inferiority was degradation, and her family and connections below his notice. Was he not the soul of gallantry to brave all that?

Gah!

Then, after every possible manner of insult, he claimed violent love?

No, a man such as he could know nothing about love.

Her pace increased. Perhaps speed would alleviate the burgeoning pressure within.

The path widened out to a grove. Was that a deer—no, it was a man, a most familiar figure of a man!

She rather encounter Old Nick himself than Mr. Darcy right now. How Mr. Collins would scold her for even thinking such a thing!

"Miss Bennet." He approached and held out a letter.

She instinctively took it. What else did one do when someone handed you something unexpected?

"I have been walking in the grove sometime in the hope of meeting you. Will you do me the honor of reading that letter?" He bowed ever so slightly, the minimum act of civility he might offer, and disappeared from sight.

His appearance was so fleeting he might have been an apparition except for the weighty missive in her trembling hands.

How dare he threaten her reputation by writing her? Better to burn the hateful thing than dare be caught with it.

He was so proper, so proud. Why would he extend such an effort aside from … from what? What could he possibly have left unsaid yesterday?

She slid her finger under the heavy wax seal. It broke with a soft little crack.

Papa had always declared her far too curious for her own good.

His handwriting was bold and regular, that of one accustomed to have his words attended.

Arrogant.

She drew a deep breath. It was dated from Rosings at eight o'clock in the morning. One could have no expectation of pleasure from a letter dated so early in the morning.

Be not alarmed, Madam, on receiving this letter, by the apprehension of its containing any repetition of those sentiments, or renewal of those offers, which were last night so disgusting to you. You must, therefore, pardon the freedom with which I demand your attention; your feelings, I know, will bestow it unwillingly, but I demand it of your justice.

Her justice?

What apology could he offer? What explanation could excuse the things he had done?

Two offences of a very different nature, and by no means of equal magnitude, you last night laid to my charge. The first, that, regardless of the sentiments of either, I had detached Mr. Bingley from your sister, and the other, that I had ruined the immediate prosperity, and blasted the prospects of Mr. Wickham.

So he had been listening to her. That was something. But he was so haughty, so arrogant. He expressed no regret for what he had done to Jane and Bingley, only ignorance as to Jane's feelings.

But as to Wickham … that she had been so certain of—it made so little sense now. She pressed her forehead with her palms and screwed her eyes shut.

Mr. Darcy agreed with so many of the particulars of Wickham's tales, their boyhood, the kindness of old Mr. Darcy, the living, too. They had to be telling two sides of the same story.

Mr. Wickham had conveniently left out the remuneration he received upon giving up the living, though. What scruples might he have about leaving out other significant information, perhaps even altering it to suit his ends? Why she had been so willing to believe him? His confidences to her—a veritable stranger—could hardly be considered appropriate. But they flattered her vanity.

She drove the heels of her hands into her eyes but it did little to stop the unsettling images flashing through her mind.

Why would Mr. Darcy have told her such an infamous story about his sister, unless it were true?

This, madam, is a faithful narrative of every event in which we have been concerned together. I shall endeavor to find some opportunity of putting this letter in your hands in the course of the morning.

I will only add, God bless you.

Her hands quivered so hard she could not have read further had there been more.

Though his offer was gallant, she did not need to consult with Colonel Fitzwilliam. Every word written had to be true, and Mr. Darcy vindicated.

She, who had prided herself on discernment, had been naught but blind, partial, prejudiced and absurd.

Until this moment she had never truly known herself.

She sank down on a tree stump and clutched her waist. How she had abused him—to others and to his face—calling into question his character, his motives, his manners. No those were certainly wanting.

Still, even that did not signify compared to the abhorrent way she treated him.

Every finer feeling in her bosom demanded repentance. Whether or not he would accept it, she must offer it.

But how? Surely he would never speak to her again. And this was certainly not information to relay through another party, no matter how trusted.

Heavy boots crunched toward her. Great heavens, he could not be returning to gloat, could he?

"Miss Bennet?"

"Colonel Fitzwilliam?"

He bowed. "I had no idea of meeting you here. How fortuitous. You are far better company than I expected to encounter."

"Dare I ask who you anticipated?"

"Dreaded would be a better word. I thought Darcy might be walking the grounds. I do not fancy his company right now. He has been in high dudgeon since yesterday. I am glad to see you though. Are you recovered from yesterday's headache?"

"Yes, thank you." She rose and dusted off her skirt, tucking Darcy's letter up the sleeve of her spencer.

His eyebrow twitched. Pray let him not have seen!

"I am sorry to hear of your cousin's discomfiture. Have you ... have you any notion as to its cause?"

Great heavens! What possessed her to ask such a question?

"None what so ever, save it sent him scurrying to his writing table. I imagine he received some unwelcome news, probably in the post." He offered his arm, and they began to walk. "If I had to guess—and since you have asked it seems I should—I expect he has heard from Georgiana. She is only sixteen and prone to such high and low spirits. Most recently some very low ones."

Poor girl, with neither mother nor sisters to confide in after such a trial. Of course she would want to talk, but surely not with a brother, especially one as severe as Mr. Darcy.

"You have younger sisters, three as I understand. Have you any notion of how one improves a young woman's spirits? I find myself at quite a loss." He scratched behind his left ear.

Oh, for someone to be so committed to the improvement of her own spirits!

"It is difficult to say, sir. I believe it would depend upon the reason for her melancholy."

"The reason? Who could know? She has everything a girl could want, and a brother who would move heaven and earth on her behalf." His tone turned a little defensive, and he squinted into a sun-beam breaking through the trees.

No doubt, Georgiana wanted for nothing, nothing save a clear conscience. Poor child. "Then perhaps it is not something she lacks, but someone."

"Do you suggest she wishes for a suitor?" He stiff-ened and glared.

"Not at sixteen, sir. At that age, a young woman is always in need of a wise, mature confidant with whom she may share the secrets of her heart."

"She has a companion."

"Although I have never enjoyed the society of a companion, I must imagine they are no different to other women. Is she sympathetic or apt to be critical?"

He pulled up a little straighter and cocked his head as though she had spoken in some unheard of foreign tongue. "I do not know."

"Then perhaps it would be worth ascertaining."

They walked several more steps across the soft dirt. His brows drew together, rose and fell, carrying on a conversation of their own.

"I would never have considered such a thing, no not at all. A very useful thought I would say. I may just write her and ask those very questions."

"I dare say she would be pleased for such a letter. Surprised, but pleased."

Colonel Fitzwilliam chuckled. "I can only hope—and I dare say with little expectation of it being borne out—that Darcy too might soon receive some cheer-ful correspondence lest he drive our aunt to distraction. I suppose it is indecorous of me to say, but he is able to do it like no one else, all the while never intending it. I confess, it would be great sport to watch if it did not mean he was so beastly unhappy." He met her gaze with a raised eyebrow.

She looked away and chewed her lower lip. "I shall hope with you that he might receive just such a communication. You must excuse me, sir. I will be missed at the parsonage for breakfast if I linger any longer." She curtsied.

"Thank you for a most enlightening conversation." He winked and sauntered away.

She turned aside. Thank heavens he did not attempt to escort her back to the parsonage!

A few more minutes in his company and he might well have begun to discern her own distress. After all, he had proven himself not insensible to the feelings of Darcy and Georgiana.

She slowed her pace. Was it wrong to have told Colonel Fitzwilliam a small falsehood? The parsonage served breakfast quite late, and her absence would remain unnoticed for hours yet. Surely such a small fabrication must be excused when one suffered such a perturbation of soul.

She wrung her hands and paced across a sunbeam shining between two great oaks. Did she dare even contemplate it?

He could hardly think worse of her for emulating his own behavior. Could he?

The breach of propriety would be far, far greater than anything she had ever considered before. The risk to her reputation!

She clutched her temples. Perhaps that would silence the roar in her ears.

Mama would be mortified; Charlotte humiliated; and Mr. Collins scandalized if she were found out. She paced three steps into the shadows. None of them might ever speak to her again. Not that Mr. Collins speeches would be such a loss, but to forfeit Charlotte's friendship—that she would repine.

What did a woman have, apart from her reputation?

She turned, suddenly blinded by a shaft of sunlight so bright it obscured her view for a moment and blinked hard.

A woman also required self-respect.

How could she live with herself, knowing the unjust pain she had caused another?

How did one right such a wrong?

Surely he must hate her now, wholly and completely. No word, written or spoken might change that inevitability. His good opinion once lost, was lost forever. At least she could try. Her character required it.

There was no choice. She must write a letter.

She sucked in a deep breath or crisp morning air. Funny how resolve had a way of cooling one's anxious flutterings into something quite firm and unbending.

She turned toward the parsonage. How could one write easily and fluidly under such a burden? The injury to her pride alone was enough to render her mute a week at least.

She summoned her resolve and remained at her writing desk, forcing pen to paper, until the missive came to its right and natural conclusion.

It was surely not the most articulate letter ever penned. A heart as heavy as hers could hardly achieve eloquence, but her meaning—should he be gracious enough to receive it—would be clear enough.

She dripped a blob of wax on the pages sealing the letter and her fate. On the surface he could be disagreeable to be sure. But beneath, there was a character she could truly respect. She dragged her sleeve across her eyes. Best not dwell on that.

Darcy paced along the library windows. How many times had he trod this path since he returning from his early morning mission? Certainly enough to wear a track in the carpet. He glanced behind him. The lack of footprints should not disappoint him, but it did.

Had his letter left as little impression on her as his boots did on the flooring?

It would probably serve him right if it did.

How could he have done such a thing? What gentleman would risk her reputation? Did it not simply prove his unfeeling lack of propriety? He linked his fingers behind his neck until the joints released with a rhythmic crackle, but the tension did not release.

If Collins found it … no, she would never be so careless. Perhaps she had already done the sensible thing and consigned it to the nearest fire. How fitting for his words to be destroyed as surely as he had ruined any chance of her accepting his offer.

The door swung open, and Fitzwilliam sauntered in with long easy stride, bits of grass and leaves still caught in his boots. His arms swung effortlessly from his shoulders, and an easy smile lit his face.

How dare Fitzwilliam be so content in his presence? What had he been doing? Certainly that expression did not come from time spent in Aunt Catherine's presence.

"You look like the very devil himself, Darcy. Best not present yourself to anyone before your valet has his way with you, or do I need to have a word with him for his slovenly work?" Fitzwilliam dropped into the nearest chair and propped one boot atop the other.

"Thank you for your concern for my appearance. I shall sack my man directly. Perhaps I should hire yours from you."

"I doubt an old soldier would be much to your liking. His language alone would be enough to send you into apoplexy." He folded his hands before his chest and chuckled. "You have not the mettle for such a servant—or for anything disruptive to your life, I think."

Darcy pulled forward on his neck. Tight muscles screamed. "What makes you a sudden expert on my life? I do not believe I asked for your input recently."

"But you should have. It is clear something has off-balanced your famed Darcy reserve. I can only imagine it has something to do with a young lady of our acquaintance."

Darcy spun on his heel, the air freezing in his lungs. How could he know?

"You are far too proud, thinking yourself beyond the understanding of mere mortals. I assure you, you are all but transparent." Fitzwilliam leaned forward, elbows on his knees. "All your melancholy centers on a young woman's ill humor, and I mean to right it."

Darcy clenched his teeth, stomach churning. "And what makes you an expert on a subject heretofore declared a mystery?"

"I consulted a genuine expert."

"Aunt Catherine has suddenly become expert in the matter, or has Anne finally found a voice?" Darcy stalked to the farthest corner.

Much safer to keep his distance lest the urge to lay hands upon Fitzwilliam return.

"Miss Bennet."

He whipped his head around so fast the room spun. "You spoke with her?"

"Indeed I have. I was fortunate enough to encounter her on my walk this morning."

Dear God, what had she said to him? He squeezed his temples.

"Most fortunate indeed. She is very easy to talk to, you know. Such a shame I have not the means to pursue her. But such is the lot of a second son's life." He shrugged, settled back into the chair and stared at him.

"What did she say?"

"It took her no time at all to understand the problem. I found her very clever indeed, and she rendered a most interesting solution. She decreed a letter should be the thing to solve it all. Upon her excellent suggestion, I have already acted to initiate the exchange. I expect you shall be receiving a communication that shall set your mind as ease quite soon."

Darcy's jaw dropped, but unable to draw breath, no words formed.

"You need not thank me. I am your oldest friend, after all, am I not? I am always solicitous after yours and Georgiana's welfare. We shall set to rights this cake of things and our lives and concerns shall return to normal." He pushed up from the chair, saluted, and strode out.

Darcy sank to the window seat, and knotted his fingers in his hair. What had Fitzwilliam done?

April 11, 1812

THE FIRST RAYS OF daylight teased her awake, though her head was muzzy and limbs filled with all the strength of sodden blankets. Good sense required she sleep a little longer, but Mr. Darcy often walked the grounds at this hour! Moreover, he would be leaving Kent on the morrow. What better reason to force herself to leave her rooms?

She tucked a tightly folded letter in the sleeve of her spencer, the place she had hidden his not a day ago, and set out. A morning fog obscured the landscape. Not the kind that faded away gently with the rays of dawn, but the kind that fought, clinging steadfastly to trees and grass, begging to be given leave to remain all day. Even if Mr. Darcy were out in it, what possibility that she might actually see him?

Her best chance lay in the place he had met her—was it just yesterday morning?

The grove had seemed so much closer yesterday, but today she was weighed down with the double burden of the fog and her letter. She traced the perimeter, once twice, thrice. The morning haze lost its battle with the sun, but a fourth circuit still failed to yield up her quarry.

Why had she even dared hope? What man in his right mind would chance encountering her again?

She trudged back to the parsonage. How was her letter to reach him?

"Lizzy! Lizzy!" Maria ran from the house. Where have you been? We hoped for your return a quarter of an hour ago."

"What do you mean? Is something wrong?"

"We had callers, from Rosings, intent on seeing you. Come." She grabbed Elizabeth's hand and pulled her into the house.

Charlotte waited for them just inside and led them to her sitting room. "My dear Eliza, we searched everywhere for you. But they would not stay any longer. Mr. Collins has accompanied them back to Rosings."

They sat around the table by the window, already set with things for tea.

Elizabeth took a cup from Charlotte. "What distinguished personages have caused such disarray? Did Lady Catherine and Miss de Bourgh call?"

"La! No, you silly thing, it was the colonel and Mr. Darcy." Maria clasped her hands and bounced. "They waited for you for over half an hour."

"It all seemed as though they had come as a take leave. You know they have already stayed in Kent a great deal longer than anyone expected." Charlotte sipped her tea.

"So they are not yet leaving?" Elizabeth turned aside. She dare not allow Charlotte to catch her eye.

"You will never guess why." Maria leaned forward and nearly upended her teacup. "Lady Catherine has crafted ever so delightful a scheme. A dinner party tonight! And we are all invited!"

"Invited or commanded?" Elizabeth's eyebrow arched. Mr. Darcy would most likely have to be commanded into company.

Charlotte glared.

"Forgive me. I should control my impertinence." But surprise and relief made it difficult. "Is not a single day very short notice upon which to conduct a dinner party? Mama requires at least a week and better two."

"When one has a staff the size of Lady Catherine's many thing are possible." Charlotte shrugged and settled back in her seat.

"The colonel and Mr. Darcy are to be in attendance as well." Maria flashed a flirtatious smile, far too reminiscent of Lydia's. "And I am ever so glad for their familiar faces, even if Mr. Darcy still frightens me so. She is inviting three other families whom we have never met."

"I found it odd the gentlemen would take such pains to ensure we knew their plans."

Elizabeth dodged Charlotte's gaze again and smoothed her skirts. "They are all politeness. I am sure they were aware of the anxiety such an event might occasion upon a young lady and wished to set Maria's mind at ease as soon as might be done."

"Perhaps." Charlotte called for the maid to bring more hot water and toast.

She had desired for an opportunity to encounter Mr. Darcy again. What a perverse fate that the opportunity should be in a room full of other company. Somehow, she would face him, with all proper manner and decorum. He deserved at least that much from her, even if her letter never reached him.

***

Surely there must be something wrong with every clock in the parsonage. Their hands all moved far too slowly. But the watch on her chatelaine agreed with Charlotte's clocks.

At least that gave her plenty of time to manage her toilette. Tonight when she might say so very little, she must communicate by every means available to her. She had to appear a gentleman's daughter, fully respectable … and fully repentant; sincere, but not servile. In short, everything she had not been but should have.

Even with careful preparations, she was ready three quarters of an hour before Lady Catherine's equipage was expected. For her penance, Mr. Collins kept company with her, expounding on the desirable virtues of timeliness.

How very ironic that Lady Catherine's coach was a quarter of an hour late.

Maria's nervous fretting over Lady Catherine's unfamiliar guests filled the carriage the whole way to Rosings. Charlotte tried to insist people in Kent were no different to those in Hertfordshire, and Maria had no reason for nerves. Mr. Collins, however, took exception and made certain to offer a full and complete correction to her flawed beliefs.

Elizabeth nodded and held the sleeve in which she had secreted her letter to Mr. Darcy very close to her waist. Why she had thought trying to give him a letter in the midst of a dinner party a good idea? Each time Mr. Collins glanced her direction, she feared he might discover her secret impropriety.

The butler showed them to the drawing room already bustling with other guests. Lady Catherine introduced them to the barrister, the knight and the landed gentleman who owned an estate second only to Pemberley, and their wives.

Elizabeth said all the right things, curtsied politely and struggled not to look at Mr. Darcy.

He returned the favor, avoiding even facing in her general direction.

She might have taken that as clear indication she should forget about the letter altogether—linger back as the party made their way to dinner and commit it to the fire. But something in the set of his shoulders, the line of his jaw, the tiny droop at the corner of his eyes spoke less of anger than resignation. Such a man might be willing to accept a letter, even if it were not the hoped for one from his sister.

"Dinner awaits us." Lady Catherine rose to lead the ladies out by rank. Elizabeth and Maria trailed behind, lowest of the party. For once, that felt a most desirable positon.

Elizabeth glanced over her shoulder.

Mr. Darcy dodged her gaze. Had he been staring after her?

"You must walk with me and give me courage for I do not know with whom I will sit tonight." Maria slipped her arm in Elizabeth's and propelled her to the dining room.

An abundance of fragrant dishes graced the dining table, leaving it almost too crowded for guests. Mama's dinners, reputed for excellence, were poor man's fare by comparison. How vexing to face such a first-rate meal with absolutely no appetite.

Dinner dragged on through three courses, her anxiety building through each. Even in her state of vexation, she could not resist some sustenance. The splendid victuals helped settle her nerves, but all her anxious flutterings returned as the final table cloth was removed and the sweet course, laid out before them.

The blancmange and the jellies only reminded her of the state of her equanimity. Their greatest virtue was immediately preceding Lady Catherine's call for the ladies to attend her in the drawing room. Had that command ever been so welcome?

Whilst they dined, the drawing room furnishings had been rearranged for the ease of the ladies who might wish to display. An elegant harp stood near the pianoforte. A substantial stack of music laid waiting on a cabinet near the pianoforte. A silhouette screen occupied a small table near the fireplace, stocked with pencils and paper. She expected her guests to be very accomplished indeed.

Amidst a lovely service of tea and biscuits, Lady Catherine inquired after the health of each of her guests, their families, and all of their acquaintances. She offered her recommendations on which tonics and apothecaries might serve them best. When the subject at last ran its course, Lady Catherine required entertainment.

"Miss Bennet, play for us. I feel certain you might amuse us sufficiently in the men's absence."

"I…I thank you for your confidence, Lady Catherine."

"Yes, yes, I am sure you are not accustomed to such praise. Do not dither on about it. Go play."

Beside her, Maria blanched and quivered. Truly though, what difference was playing in one company or another. She would show Maria, Kent was indeed little different to Hertfordshire. Elizabeth rose and walked to the pianoforte in calm measured steps.

The instrument was far finer than any she had ever played. Though she could not do it justice she might provide sufficient distraction for those attending to Lady Catherine's monologue.

The music distracted her as well. When had the gentlemen returned to the drawing room?

Heavens! Mr. Darcy approached. Her fingers tangled over a chord.

He stopped several steps away, his every limb rigid and face etched into a mask she had once mistaken for displeasure. "Forgive me, Miss Bennet. Colonel Fitzwilliam suggested you might require someone to turn pages for you. He intended to do the task himself, but Anne required his immediate attention, and he sent me in his stead."

She stammered meaningless syllables.

"I shall go if you prefer."

"I …ah…yes, please…that is I would be pleased for your assistance."

The hard lines on his forehead eased a mite. He stationed himself beside the pianoforte,

For the moment, just this moment he was near. They had a tiny bit of privacy, perhaps the only one they would ever have.

She came to the end of the piece. Polite applause commensurate with her middling performance followed.

"Please, sir, would you bring me the top sheet of music from the cabinet? I believe it might convey a pleasing sentiment." She forced the words out, but only managed a whisper.

His brows creased his forehead in a little 'v' she had seen many times before. Pray let him not refuse!

He tipped his head and stepped away.

She slipped the letter from her sleeve. It could tuck in just behind the sheet on the music stand. Her hands shook so hard she knocked both to the floor. Gasping, she reached for it, and her hand collided with Mr. Darcy's.

"Pray excuse me, sir." She pulled away and held her breath.

Surely he saw the letter—his name emblazoned across the front was near impossible to miss. Would he take it? He must. If anyone else found it now and read it—oh what had she done? Bad enough to risk her own reputation, but his as well? Foolish head-strong girl—

He picked up the letter along with the scattered music, only the barest twitch of his brow revealing his complicity. "Allow me to arrange this for you."

He readied the music on the stand, her letter barely visible, concealed in his broad palm. He had not left it behind!

She peeked up at him, but his face was the same impassive mask he usually wore. Then again, that was a good sign. His ire, when raised, was always quite apparent.

"Was this the music you desired?" He glanced at the music stand.

"Yes…thank you."

Bother how could she have forgotten to play? She squinted at the music and willed her fingers to the keys. They obeyed, only stumbling over a few bars.

Civil applause reminded her it was finished. She managed to walk back to her seat, though she felt like a wobbly kneed calf taking its first steps.

Mr. Darcy strode to Lady Catherine. What was he saying to her—no, he was leaving! She bit her knuckle. Had she offended so desperately—or perhaps, was it possible?

Did he go to read her letter?

Or maybe to destroy it.

How he hated disguise of every sort, yet the falsehood he told Aunt Catherine was utterly and entirely necessary. If he did not escape the drawing room, he would surely run mad. A brisk walk to the stable to check on his horse, who was most certainly not unwell, would cool his humors and settle his nerves.

He pressed his hand to his pocket. Sharp corners drove into his ribs. Yes, it was still there.

Why did Fitzwilliam send him to her? Had Anne truly waylaid him on his way to assist, or was it some darker plan? What was he about?

Had the lady not sufficiently abused him enough to his face?

Had you behaved in a more gentleman-like manner …

Oh, those words would never leave him. She was right. What sounded so reasonable, so well-considered in the sanctity of his own mind turned cold and unfeeling when spoken aloud.

What a fool he was to give voice to the violence of his feelings.

The evening air filled his lungs, cooling his chest and bracing his resolve. She, it seemed, had done him the courtesy of reading his letter—what else could explain the missive now in his pocket?

The night boasted a full moon, but while enough to light the road, it would not support reading a lady's hand. He stopped beside one of the torches, flickering and popping beside the lane to the manor. The smell of the heat tickled his nose as he withdrew the letter from his pocket. The light danced across his name, teasing, daring him to open it.

He steeled himself. Surely he had only added to his catalogue of offences by writing to her. Certainly that merited her rebuke.

Even so, he had to read it. If for no other reason than to honor the risk she took in writing to him. A gentleman would.

Still, nothing in her countenance suggested that might be her purpose. Might it be possible … no, hope was naught but a fool's errand. It would be sufficient if she no longer impugned his character.

Barely trembling, clumsy fingers cracked the wax seal. Bits of it tumbled into the darkness, disappearing into the shadows.

Be not alarmed, good sir, on receiving this letter, by the apprehension that it will contain a repetition of sentiments we both would prefer to forget.

Your thorough and candid communication has not fallen upon deaf ears. I will not soon forget the intelligence you shared with me. I beg that you would therefore pardon the freedom with which I have demanded your attention, but my character requires it.

Her voice, gentle and soft, spoke the words in his mind, barely audible over the deafening roar of blood in his ears. That she did not abuse him at the start was a good sign, but no assurance she did not still regard him a bounder. A ragged breath braced him for more.

You willingly acknowledge your errors with regards to my sister's sentiments toward Mr. Bingley. I can do no less.

After carefully weighing the evidence provided me by Mr. Wickham, yourself, and unwittingly by Col. Fitzwilliam, and considering your willingness to direct me to him for further corroboration of your facts, I realize my judgements concerning Mr. Wickham have been gravely flawed.

The manner by which he imposed his falsehood upon me is irrelevant. I am now deeply aware of the true nature of your dealings with him. And his with you.

A breath he did not recognize he had held escaped in a painful rush. His knees threatened to buckle, and he grabbed the torch. Its meager support barely kept him on his feet. That and the knowledge she no longer indicted him for Wickham's misfortune.

Why that should matter so much? He wiped beads of sweat from his brow.

I cannot, though, condone your interference with my sister's happiness. I see now that it was done for genuine concern for Mr. Bingley's welfare, if carried out in pride and high handedness. These are motives which I cannot condemn.

Good motives, though, do not serve to mend ruined hopes and happiness. I fear the recovery from her disappointed affections will be long in coming. For that I struggle to forgive you.

However when I consider what my own behavior has been, I appreciate the hypocrisy of clinging to my resentment.

Acid rose in his throat and burned the back of his tongue. He had expected her rebuke, but not like this. She was right. Right and proper motives did nothing to excuse the damage he had inflicted. Was Bingley as affected as Miss Bennet? He had lost his usual enthusiasm for social engagements after being persuaded of Miss Bennet's indifference.

Perhaps Darcy had been wrong to accept it as a welcome change from Bingley's usual exuberance. Could it be a sign of true despondency?

London should be his next stop from Rosings. Bingley would still be in residence there.

You are fortunate to have so little to repine in regards to the whole affair. I however find several areas upon which I cannot look at my own behavior with satisfaction. Although I have prided myself in good judgement, I failed to exercise it in evaluating Mr. Wickham's representations of your character. This lead to what causes me the greatest grief. I maligned and abused the character of a man who has proved to be very much the opposite of what I believed him to be.

For that I am truly and deeply remorseful.

Zounds!

How neatly her contrition delivered another blow to his pride. He should have better acknowledged his error to her, apologized as freely as she. Her captivating humility put him to shame. Strong and forthright, it only reminded him of his undiminished regard for her.

In another matter though, I must beg to be acquitted. Please believe me when I tell you, your offer to me came as a complete surprise. I had not the slightest indication of the feelings you proclaimed. Taken by surprise as I was, my character demands that I must have refused.

I do not regret my refusal, therefore. But it will forever pain me that I should have done so in so unfeeling a manner as to render impossible any future friendship between us. I shall always look upon that with regret.

No idea of his regard? How was that possible? He threw his head back and stared into the moon-bright sky. Were not his regular visits to the parsonage, his attentions to her conversation, his lingering glances enough to assure any woman of his affections?

He shoved the letter into his pocket and stalked into the darkness.

Willful, stubborn woman, what did she expect from him? Bingley-like declarations and effusions of sentiment dripping about like treacle on porridge?

He snorted. He was no more capable of that than he was of taking flight. Such expectations were entirely unreasonable.

But was that what she expected? Did she expect anything at all?

She is tolerable; but not handsome enough to tempt me…

He cringed. What woman would have entertained expectations after hearing herself described thus? Arrogant, stupid fool! He dragged his hand down his face. No wonder Bingley had been so disgusted with him that night.

Of course she would not regret her refusal under such circumstances. But she regretted the loss of his friendship? His heart began beating again and his chest burned.

He sought out the torch light and unfurled the missive.

If your abhorrence of me should make my assertions valueless, I understand and cannot hold that against you. I will only add, God bless you.

She offered him blessings. Of all people, she would not offer such a thing idly any more than he.

Could it be?

He ran for the manor.

———✦———

Until this evening, Elizabeth had overlooked one very real advantage to an evening in Lady Catherine's drawing room. One had the opportunity to enjoy fine surrounds and excellent victuals without having to supply much in the way of actual conversation. As long as one appeared to listen, Lady Catherine remained quite content. With her mind in its current state of perturbation, nothing she could have offered would have resembled sense, so it was just as well her comments remained unrequired.

Movement at the drawing room doorway caught Elizabeth's eye. Darcy strode in with only a faint trickle of sweat down the side of his face and a lock of hair fallen over his forehead to suggest his state of mind.

Oh! He had not been so disarranged even the afternoon he had made his offer to her! Where had he gone, and who had left him in this condition?

Great heavens, he approached! She held her breath as he took a seat beside Colonel Fitzwilliam.

Lady Catherine turned to him with the greatest of condescension. "So, Darcy, you have returned. How is this prized horse of yours that would deprive us of your company?"

"The creature turned up a bit lame, it seems. It would be best to further delay our departure for several more days whilst it recovers." He glanced at the colonel, one eyebrow lifted just a mite.

The colonel blinked slowly.

They must have been communicating like this nearly all their lives. Not unlike she and Jane.

"Welcome news," Lady Catherine said. "I believe nobody feels the loss of friends so much as I do." She raised her hands toward Mr. Darcy and the colonel. "I am particularly attached to these nephews of mine; and know them to be so much attached to me! I recall you were excessively sorry to go last year! I knew you would feel it even more acutely this year. I know your attachment to Rosings must certainly increase with each visit. ."

Mr. Darcy formed his features into something which neither agreed nor disagreed.

She must commit that particular expression to memory. It could certainly be useful in dealing with Mama.

"And you, Miss Elizabeth Bennet, how do you find Rosings? You seem a great deal out of spirits this evening."

"I thank you for your attentions, madam. I … I was just reflecting upon my mother's last letter to me. She wrote to hurry my return."

Mr. Darcy twitched and looked her way, brows drawn over his eyes. How very expressive he was when one took the care to observe him.

"But if that is the case, you must write to your mother to beg that you may stay a little longer. Mrs. Collins will be very glad of your company, I am sure."

So she commanded the extent of Charlotte's hospitality as well? That really should not come as such a surprise.

"I am much obliged to your ladyship for your kind invitation, but it is not in my power to accept it—I am expected to be in town next Saturday."

"Why, at that rate, you will have been here only six weeks. I expected you to stay two months complete. There can be no occasion for your going so soon. Mrs. Bennet could certainly spare you for another fortnight."

"But my father cannot."

Darcy's expression darkened further.

"Oh! Your father of course may spare you, if your mother can. Daughters are never of so much consequence to a father. And if you will stay another month complete, it will be in my power to take you as far as London, for I am going there early in June, for a week; and as Dawson does not object to the Barouche box, there will be very good room for you—especially as you are neither of you are large."

"I…I do not know, madam." She bit her upper lip and chanced a peek at Darcy.

Darcy started, but recovered quickly. "I am in agreement with my aunt. I cannot imagine it proper for young women to travel post by themselves."

"Indeed not!" Lady Catherine's face flushed and leaned forward just a bit. "I have the greatest dislike in the world for that sort of thing. Young women should always be properly guarded and attended, according to their situation in life. When my niece Georgiana went to Ramsgate last summer, I made a point of her having two men servants go with her. Miss Darcy, the daughter of Mr. Darcy of Pemberley, and Lady Anne, could not have appeared with propriety in a different manner. I am excessively attentive to all those things."

Elizabeth's jaw dropped and her eyes widened. Colonel Fitzwilliam sat very straight and Mr. Darcy winced.

Mr. Darcy cleared his throat and tapped his pocket. "I am sure it would be most pleasant to ride in Lady Catherine's barouche. As I understand it is newly sprung. Perhaps even as agreeable as walking the grounds of Rosings on a lovely spring morning."

The arms of her chair nearly cried out as she clutched them.

"Indeed you are right, Darcy. When the top of the barouche is down, it is quite refreshing and ever so much more amenable to Anne's delicate health. I do, though, highly recommend walking for one's constitution. There is nothing like it for strengthening the body and soul."

He held her gaze, he nodded. "A brisk morning walk is, I believe, one of the best ways to begin a day. Would you not agree, Miss Bennet?"

Something about the way he said her name sent prickles down her back and along her arms. Had anyone else noticed?

Mr. Collins sat poised to catch each word Lady Catherine might say. Maria nodded frantically, in case she might miss the need to do so. But Charlotte's eyebrow lifted, just a mite.

"I…yes, of course, sir. You are correct. There is nothing like a footpath through a grove lined with old roses and a scattering of primrose."

"Only improved if there were a view of a fine trout stream perhaps?"

"There you go, thinking only of your sport." Lady Catherine sniffed. "Young men are so single minded in their pursuits of amusement."

Lady Catherine continued, but Elizabeth lost track of the conversation. She knew a spot exactly as he described.

April 12, 1812

ELIZABETH STARED AT THE clock's hands as they made their agonizingly slow trek around the clock face. If only she could sleep to make the time pass faster. But one did not sleep when her mind churned faster than a galloping horse's hooves.

What if she were wrong? Perhaps he meant none of those things she thought she had heard. After all, she had greatly misjudged him, not once, but many times already.

She rolled up and pressed her back against the cold headboard. The uneven carvings dug into her back. Tucking her knees under her chin, she drew the blankets around her.

How she had mistreated him, misunderstood what was going on around her, misrepresented the transgressions of her family as harmless foibles. Foolish headstrong girl!

Perhaps she should embroider that on a pillow for her room that she might never forget. Not that such anguish of soul might be easily forgotten.

Pink rays of dawn beckoned at the window sill and she sprang from her bed. Enough, enough, enough! She was not formed for idleness. Now she might dress, and walk, and return to write her father and beg he insist upon her quick return. Lady Catherine would have to accede to his wishes.

She donned a plain gown and formed a simple knot with her hair. Entirely appropriate for a morning ramble during which she would see and talk to no one.

Morning mist slapped wetly at her cheeks. In an hour, even half it would lose its unpleasant thickness and be merely a refreshing reminder of the early hour. But she could not wait that long and perhaps miss—

No, she would miss nothing. No one. This was a typical morning walk, alone.

The footpath leading to the grove of old roses and primroses near the trout stream opened up before her. In her time at Rosings, it had become one of her favorite treks. But today …

Today was no different than any other day, and she would do as she purposed.

There, in the shadows of a large oak! But it was…yes it was. Those shoulders, hands clasped behind him, the turn of his booted calf. It could be none other.

She froze. Her feet screamed for her to leave, to run. But in which direction? She looked before her and behind.

Too late! Long purposed strides brought him to her faster that she thought possible.

"Miss Bennet." He bowed, stiff and proper.

"Mr....Mr. Darcy." She attempted a curtsey, but nearly stumbled.

His jaw worked but no actual words formed. He huffed and stared at the sky. "I am not an eloquent man."

"Perhaps you should have written another letter."

He chuckled, an utterly unfamiliar, but very pleasing sound. Who would have expected that?

"Would you care to walk?" He gestured down the footpath.

Perhaps he was right. Somehow it was far easier to talk whilst moving.

"I am gratified you read my letter and did not simply burn it." He stared straight ahead, his face obscured by the dappled shade.

"As am I that you have read mine. I would not at all have blamed you for destroying it without a second thought. Pray sir, allow me to say how deeply I regret—"

"What did you say that I did not deserve, and richly so? 'Had you behaved in a more gentleman like manner ...' I cannot tell you how that rebuke has tormented me."

"Had I any expectation my words would be received so—"

"I can imagine you considered me devoid of any proper feeling. You must have believed me capable of ignoring them completely. I shudder to think what else you supposed me capable of."

"I was very wrong to impugn your character."

"Perhaps so, but I recognize my manners are apt to invite censure. I have neither the skills nor the open temper society finds agreeable." He looked up into the trees.

"I had no idea you found my advice so valuable, sir. I confess my surprise."

"Much as your surprise when I came to see you at the parsonage?" He hesitated for two heartbeats and walked on.

"Pray do not remind me of what I said then. It was entirely insupportable, regardless of my surprise. I must compliment you on your own self-control in the face of my wholly indecorous display."

He cast a sidelong glance her way. "I suppose neither of us has shown ourselves to greatest advantage, have we?"

"I did not realize you had a penchant for understatement."

"You were truly unaware of my regard for you?" He stopped and looked down at her.

How very tall he was ... and handsome.

"I cannot express my complete shock when you revealed the violence of your feelings."

"You wound my pride, Miss Bennet, but rightfully so, I expect. I considered only myself, my feelings, and the great pleasure I expected such an announcement to occasion."

Was that a note of irony in his very somber tone?

"I suppose you expected a lady to be so excited by the prospect as to ignore the manner of your declaration and possibly her own feelings on the matter."

He kicked a clump of dirt, shattering it into a cloud of dust. "I suppose I did. Much as you relied upon your own superior sense and judgment to sketch my character."

"I must grant you your point, sir."

"You are very generous, madam." He walked on, eyes firmly on the ground.

With each step, the knots in her shoulders tightened. The air turned so brittle, it might shatter, but he continued on in silence.

They approached the edge of the trout stream. Several fat fish swam past, fighting their way around a strong current that would have stranded them in a shallow backwater, an invitation to whatever predator might come.

"So what is there to be done? It seems rather a hopeless cause." He balanced his foot on a largish rock and leaned forward on his knee, peering into the stream.

She crouched and dangled her fingers in the current. "You see that trout, the big one. He is standing sentinel at this place, helping the smaller fish to stay their course. See how he chases some out of this spot, almost as though urging them to begin their journey again."

He moved behind her, a tangible presence, imposing and yet sheltering. Leaning over her shoulder, he hunkered down beside her.

"I see the one you mean. He might be the same wily old fish Fitzwilliam and I dreamt of catching in our boyhood. The one that always outsmarted us."

"I cannot see you outwitted by a mere fish."

"No, I shall not be." He stood and offered her his hand.

She took it. How strong and sure his grasp. With a deep breath, she raised her eyes and stared into the face of a man she had never seen before. His eyes, they spoke of feelings that matched his declarations. The turn of his lips, was it just a little shy and uncertain? He bore some resemblance to the Master of Pemberley whose acquaintance she had made, but he must be some distant, and very attractive, relation.

"I am very pleased to make your acquaintance, Miss Bennet." He bowed. "I understand you are to be staying another fortnight in Hunsford?"

"Ah, yes, sir, I am. And I am pleased to make your acquaintance as well." She curtsied, a little off balance.

Mr. Darcy smiled.

Oh, the power of that expression. Perhaps it was a very good thing indeed he did not do so more often. It was a shame though he had not done so sooner. Such an expression she would never have misunderstood.

"I am pleased to hear it. I shall be here a fortnight more before traveling to London to share some important intelligence with a good friend there."

She gasped.

"Until that time, would you permit me to show you around Rosings Park? You might acquaint yourself with its finer qualities?" He offered her his arm.

She had seen men try to be charming before, and this was not it. It lacked the polish, the sophistication, the genteel veneer. No this was unpracticed, tentative, and so very real, as real as the hard strength of his arm beneath her hand. An offering of peace, and perhaps of hope.

"You are very gracious, sir. I am most anxious to better know the character and sensibilities of this most intriguing landscape."

She took his arm and they walk off the established path, into the sunrise.

Last Dance

Chapter 1

TO BE FOND OF dancing was a certain step towards falling in love. Mary was not. Nor was she fond of dresses or balls or parties, or any of the things most girls her age adored.

Which was precisely why she stood in Aunt Philips' dressing room, trying on the fourth gown of the morning.

"Stand up straight! You must attend to your posture. Really, Mary, I do not understand. Why are you not more pleased that Jane and Elizabeth left you so many of their old dresses?" Aunt Phillips tugged the bodice of the calico walking dress and peered at Mary's image in the mirror.

Why did she do that? Surely it would be more effective to look at her directly, without the odd waves and shadows the imperfect looking glass imparted.

"Does not Lydia have far greater need than I? As I understand her circumstances—"

"Her circumstances are her own doing, whatever your mother tells you. She should be made to feel them all. Besides, dear, she is married and you are not. You have far greater need of finery than Lydia." Aunt Philips fiddled with the drawstring to adjust the neckline.

"Kitty then—"

"Kitty got her fair share. Do not fear! She took all she could carry with her to London. I still do not understand why you chose not to accompany them to Mr. Bingley's house in town. He is well connected. Those connections can put both of you in the way of meeting other rich young men. I say, I have scarce met a girl who dislikes dresses and beaus as you do."

Any sensible girl, when confronted with sisters lovelier, livelier, cleverer and more agreeable than she would come to the same conclusion. New clothes always came at a price: lectures and demeaning remarks regarding every aspect of her person. She shuddered.

"Do be still child, or I will stab you with a pin." Aunt Phillips spoke without looking up from the bottom of the skirt. "It is a grand thing Jane is so much taller than you. It gives me enough fabric to put a lovely set of tucks in this skirt."

"You could just allow me to pull up all the extra and restitch the waist. I do not mind the effort at all. It would be so much more straightforward."

"And far less fashionable. Your gowns may not be new, but I will see that they reflect well on us all."

Mary looked at the ceiling. At least a walking dress she could make some use of. This exercise would not be entirely in vain.

"After we finish this one, I have in mind for you to try that lovely white muslin. Some might remember it as Lizzy's. But you and I, working together, should be able to embellish it with something lovely. We can surely make it your own in time for the Michaelson's Midsummer's Day ball."

Mary clutched her forehead and pressed her lips hard. "I told you; I am not going."

"Do not be contrary with me, young lady. Your family was invited. With the rest of your family off visiting Jane, you are the only one left to go. You cannot disregard the invitation without causing offense to Mrs. Michaelson. You must do your duty."

"And what is my duty?"

"To your community: to attend the ball and set an example for proper behavior and decorum. To your family: find yourself a husband so you do not burden them with your upkeep."

Mary's stomach hardened into a painful knot around those harsh words. It always came back to that ugly truth. A girl too poor to support herself enjoyed painfully few choices apart from marriage. No doubt her brothers, not Wickham of course, but Darcy and Bingley would help her. Still, the life of a dependent relative promised to be distasteful at best.

Perhaps it was time to harden herself to the reality of her situation. Like Charlotte Lucas, she had to marry before she became an affliction to the rest of her family.

Aunt Philips' efforts were all in hope of a better future for her. How ungrateful for her to continue fighting Aunt at every turn.

"Here, now, try this one. It was one of Lizzy's. I think it will require less alteration."

Mary shrugged off the calico and slipped on the white muslin. The soft, sheer fabric coursed like cool water over her skin. The gossamer textile was far finer than Mama had ever allowed her. Such beautiful things would have been wasted on her plainest child. Perhaps it would be easier to attend a ball in such a lovely gown.

"I say, the dress becomes you. Who knew you had quite as fine a figure as Lizzy? Why ever do you hide it underneath all those shawls and fichus?"

Mary colored. Was it wrong to wish a man to look at her face rather than her décolletage?

"It will only take a moment to pin in the adjustments. Then I want you to dress for dinner. We are expecting guests tonight."

She must not roll her eyes. What should it matter that she was in no mood for company? Gardiner women were excellent hostesses and the whole of the county enjoyed their hospitality. But surely there were limits, were there not? Aunt Philips had taken it as her personal mission to invite every unmarried man in Hertfordshire for dinner or cards in the course of just two months. Would it really hurt not to host guests for a whole week complete?

Mary paused at the top of the stairs and tugged the sleeves of Jane's blue dinner dress. It still felt more like a costume for a mask than a frock of her own.

She closed her eyes and let her head drop back against the wall. A masquerade described this all so perfectly: Mama and Aunt Philips molding her to play the role of a woman who would be a social asset to her husband. Beautiful as Jane, clever as Lizzy, and as full of lively conversation as Lydia. All the things she was not. Bad enough to perform the part night after night for dinner guests, what would happen if she succeeded?

Suppose she charmed a man and convinced him to marry her? Surely, she could not maintain the façade forever. What would happen when he discovered her true nature? How could he not but hate her for her duplicity?

She clutched the banister, swallowing back the bitter taste. What choice did she have? While Jane and Lizzy had seen their romantic notions come to fruition, that outcome was hardly likely for one as dull and plain as herself.

Still, an amiable match and a husband with whom she might enjoy a friendship would be very pleasing. But friendship could not be built upon a foundation of deceit.

She straightened her spine. There was only one thing to do for it. She must acquire one more accomplishment to complete her preparation for married life. She would follow Mama's and Aunt Philips' instruction and not just play the role, but become the perfect social asset. Yet, she would allow some part of her true self to peek through…her taste in books and music.

Surely that would not be unacceptable. If she could keep just that much of herself, then she could…she would play the role demanded of her.

The front door creaked open and unfamiliar voices wafted up the stairway. Whatever else they discussed tonight, her favorite poetry would be among the topics. Now, she would face their guests.

"Mary dear, do join us." Tiny creases appeared at the sides of Aunt Philip's eyes as she waved Mary into the parlor.

Mary pressed her lips—how kind of her to draw so much attention to her arrival. Heaven forbid Aunt attempt to understand just how very difficult this was for her. But Mama did the same thing, so why should she expect it to be different here?

Aunt Philips sighed exactly the same way Mama did. "Mary, may I introduce Mr. Giles Lacey. Mr. Lacey, Miss Mary Bennet."

A tall, well-looking young man stood and bowed. His fine jacket barely fastened over his broad chest. He must have chosen breeches instead of trousers to show off his fine calves. He tied his cravat less than perfectly though, so he was no fop.

He bowed. "Most pleased to make your acquaintance."

She curtsied, heart fluttering more than she would have cared to admit. His hair, his eyes and his smile—

"Mr. Lacey has just taken over the old Oliver farm."

"Indeed? How do you find it? Has it not been vacant for near a year now?" Mary asked.

"Sufficient, for the time being. Over the coming years, I hope to acquire the two adjacent properties. That should make a proper estate of it."

She closed her eyes briefly. "I do believe the three together would be nearly the size of Longbourn, my father's estate. You have a most ambitious plan."

"Excuse me, but I am quite certain it would be smaller, by about twenty percent." The other man in the room stood.

Mr. Lacey guffawed. "You must forgive my cousin, Parris. He is such a stickler for accuracy. Never willing to accept an estimate when precise numbers might be named."

Mr. Parris rose to his full, substantial height and brought his cane down with a clatter. He limped two steps toward them, an odd hopping gait reminiscent of a grasshopper. His face was long and gaunt, but his eyes bespoke a gentle temperament behind his curt words.

"You could introduce me." Mr. Parris grumbled under his breath.

Mr. Lacey bowed from his shoulders and gestured toward Mr. Parris. "My cousin, Parris, who has just completed his course at Oxford. He has come to live with me and work for your uncle."

"So you are to be uncle's new clerk?" Mary curtsied.

"We have yet to finalize the entire agreement, but yes, that is the intention."

Mr. Lacey cuffed Mr. Parris' shoulder. "Never one to offer a simple 'yes' when one hundred words of explanation might do instead."

Mr. Parris tugged his lapels. "Odd, how you never appreciate my precision until you want your books balanced or a contract written."

"Lacey! Parris!" Uncle Philips bustled into the room. "So glad you could join us tonight. No doubt you could use a decent meal. Bachelors never eat so well as when they are the guests of a good hostess."

"We appreciate your gracious invitation." Mr. Lacey smiled again.

Mary's pulse skipped and tripped over its own rhythm. His eyes sparkled when he laughed.

"Shall we repair to the dining room?" Aunt Philips asked.

Mr. Lacey offered Mary his arm.

Gracious! No one had ever escorted her in to dinner before. She slipped her hand into the crook of his arm. Mr. Parris followed them in, cane clicking along the hard wood as he went.

Aunt's dining room was smaller and plainer than Mama's at Longbourn. But a house in town was rarely as fine as a country estate—so Mama insisted. There was much to be said for a tastefully appointed, cozy room, though. After all, Mr. Collins had remarked on its resemblance to one of the lesser rooms at Rosings.

Mary bit her lip. Aunt would notice if she laughed aloud. The comment was still a sore point with Aunt Philips. She still wondered whether to consider it a compliment or not, despite Mr. Collins' protestations.

Mr. Lacey seated Mary between her uncle and himself with his cousin across from them both. Uncle Philips did the honors at the foot of the table, carving a roast joint of mutton. Aunt Philips announced the cauliflower, collops of veal smothered in onions, mashed potatoes with bacon, pea soup and mixed-fruit pie.

Fragrant, plentiful, but rather plain. Did Aunt count on bachelors being easily impressed to economize on tonight's meal? She had been doing a great deal of entertaining recently.

Mary squirmed in her seat. Should she be impressed or embarrassed? The Gouldings would have rated two courses with removes.

"Would you care for potatoes, Miss Bennet?" Mr. Lacey asked, depositing a spoonful before she could reply.

Luckily, she did want a bit of everything that appeared upon her plate without her consent. It was pleasant to be served so attentively, though perhaps not in such great quantities. Obviously, Mr. Lacey had never heard Mama's lectures that a lady should eat sparingly in company.

"So, Lacey, how is it you came to Hertfordshire," Uncle Philips handed the platter of carved mutton to Mr. Parris.

"It was Parris' fault, really."

Mr. Parris touched his forehead in a small salute. "Always pleased to be of service to any of my kith or kin."

"True enough—I have never known a fellow quicker to offer assistance than you. You had only just spoken with Philips about the clerkship when you wrote to me about the Oliver place. Thought it was precisely the situation for me, and I agreed."

"If your interest was in clerking for my uncle, how came you to know about the farm?" Mary asked.

Mr. Parris' cheeks colored just a bit. "I make it a point to research my surroundings—"

"And just about everything else." Mr. Lacey cocked an eyebrow.

Mr. Parris cleared his throat. "Thorough research is an indulgence that often serves me well."

"It certainly makes for an excellent solicitor." Uncle Phillips nodded. "So you have some experience in farming, Lacey?"

"Worked the farm with my father until he died last spring. My elder brother then took over the family farmstead. Father left me enough that, with my own savings, I could purchase a yeoman's farm of my own.

I moved in with Parris and have been watching for a suitable place ever since."

"Well, it is good to know someone who knows his business will be taking over." Aunt dabbed her lips with her napkin. "Mr. Oliver made quite the mess out of everything, I would say."

Mary grimaced. Though it was true, Mr. Oliver had never seen a wholly successful harvest, Aunt Philips would hardly hold bad weather and worse drainage against someone. No, her rancor stemmed from his failure to appreciate her invitations to dine with them.

Mrs. Goulding had informed her Mr. Oliver considered her a droll hostess at best. Worse, he accused her of not paying her cook enough, and allowing inferior dishes on her table. Since then, Aunt Philips never seemed to bypass an opportunity to criticize the poor man. Mr. Lacey chuckled.

Mary's cheeks flushed and prickled. "I dare say farming is a chancy business at best. One can never plan for all the vagaries of weather and calamities that may strike. One must look to Providence—"

"I would rather count on hard work and good planning." Mr. Lacey's brows rose just a bit.

Mary squirmed in her seat and turned to Mr. Parris. "So how did you come to know my uncle needed a clerk?"

"I have a friend who teaches at Oxford, He recommended Parris to me. Old Scott thinks highly of you," Uncle Philips raised his glass toward Mr. Parris.

"Is that the old man with the weak arm and the brogue so thick his speech barely sounds like the King's English?" Mr. Lacey attempted his own brogue.

Mr. Parris pressed his lips into something not quite a frown. "He is a brilliant teacher and an excellent man."

"That may be so," Mr. Lacey leaned his elbow on the table. "But it brutalizes a man's hearing to listen to him go on and on. You cannot deny it."

Mr. Parris turned aside.

"It must be a very pleasant thing that both of you are coming together so you will have someone you know here. I can only imagine how difficult it would be to go somewhere without any acquaintance," Mary said softly.

"A change of scenery can be a very pleasant thing indeed." Mr. Lacey said.

"Of course it can, you silly girl." Aunt Philips shoved her napkin under the side of plate. "You must forgive her, you see her elder sisters are lately married and gone from home. Though they are splendidly matched—"

Mary turned her head and dropped her gaze to her lap. What did Aunt Philips want from her? Was it not enough that she was trying to participate in the conversation? It was not necessary to publicly put her quiet disposition on trial and deem it wanting once again.

"A lady moved far from home must be one unhappy with her lot?" Mr. Lacey's brows rose. "I believe it quite possible to be far from home and yet in good spirits. This evening is quite the example of that. We have shared a lovely meal and I anticipate further diversions yet to come. I am certain our hostess would agree."

"Indeed I do, sir." She glowered at Mary.

"So what amusements are most enjoyed here in Meryton? Do you play the pianoforte? Sing, dance? Play games of cards? I myself am fond of them all."

"Then let us adjourn to the drawing room for any or all of those diversions." Aunt Philips rose.

A polite lady did not sigh, so Mary bit her lips, and the urge passed. No doubt she would be expected to play and sing. Not long ago, she would have been pleased to oblige. But after Miss Bingley's performance at Lucas Lodge and the shocking, humiliating realization that followed, she preferred to keep her meager talents to herself. Perhaps one day, if she practiced enough, she might perform for an audience again.

How could she refuse Aunt Philips when she asked though? Supper soured in her belly. How mortifying to play before these gentlemen! She dragged her feet all the way to the drawing room.

Aunt took pride in her drawing room, a showplace of her good taste and style. Every other room in the house endured economy, so she could display here. The compliments she received from her guests seemed to validate her choices, though Mary would not have complained for a bit more comfort in the private rooms.

"I say, Miss Bennet, I fancy nothing more after a nice meal than a bit of a dance. Would you oblige me?" Mr. Lacey bowed and offered his hand.

"I … but how, sir?"

"Play us something merry, Parris, a jig perhaps."

"Is that to your liking, Mrs. Philips?" Parris tipped his head slightly.

"It is a bit irregular, I must say. I thought perhaps Mary would…"

Mary gulped and looked away.

"Nonsense!" Uncle Philips pulled a pair of chairs toward the walls, clearing the center of the room. "I should enjoy a turn with you, and it would be most awkward for us to dance alone."

"Quite right. It is settled then." Mr. Lacey helped Uncle shift several pieces of furniture and led her to the center of the room.

Mr. Parris played an opening chord, and they took their places. How long had it been since she had danced with any but the dance master and her sisters in Longbourn's drawing room? There she was a welcome partner for practicing new steps. Everywhere else, she might as well bring a book. Feigning interest in the pages made the rejection sting far less.

Mr. Lacey proved a nimble, gay partner. His skill at smoothing over others' missteps transformed the experience into something entirely memorable. With a partner like him, it was easy to see why so many girls were absolutely wild for a dance.

Mr. Lacey passed her, back-to-back. "I have heard the Michaelson's of Granbury Hall are hosting a Midsummer's Day ball. Mrs. Michaelson just sent 'round an invitation to us. I imagine you have been invited as well?"

"Indeed we have, sir." Aunt Philips took his hands for a two-hand turn, "and look forward to attending."

She had only been talking constantly of it for the last fortnight.

"Then, I shall look forward to dancing with both you and your lovely niece that night." Mr. Lacey extended his hands for a circle right, once and a half around.

"I rarely dance at such events any more, but I am sure Mary…" Aunt Philips' eyebrows rose high on her forehead.

How did she do that and not lose count of where she was? Perhaps she relied on Mr. Lacey, who seemed entirely assured of what he was doing.

Mary flushed, more than the active dance engendered. "I am honored, sir…I should be pleased to dance with you that evening."

The music closed, and they honored their partners with bows and curtsies and the musician with applause.

"Capital! Parris, play us another." Mr. Lacey waved in Mr. Parris's direction.

Mr. Parris did not look up from the pianoforte, but something in the carriage of his shoulders bespoke irritation. Still, a light, lovely song poured from the keyboard.

After the second dance, Uncle Philips begged exhaustion. Aunt Philips called for tea and biscuits. Mr. Parris joined them around the tea table.

Aunt fluttered her best fan before her face. "Mr. Lacey, you are an excellent dancer—"

"Where did I learn such accomplishment, for you would not have expected such from a mere farmer?"

Aunt Philips gasped. "I meant nothing of the sort!"

His eyes twinkled, and he chuckled. "Fear not, I take no offense. You are not the first to have asked. I have three younger sisters of my own and Parris' two sisters who grew up with us. A partner for practice was always in high demand."

The housekeeper bustled in with the tea tray.

"Of course, I see." Aunt served tea. "And you Mr. Parris?"

Uncle cleared his throat, forehead creased. At least he did not roll his eyes. He had a bad habit of doing that, probably learned from Papa.

Mr. Parris touched his cane. "I shall never take to the dance floor, madam. Hence, I learnt to play to take my share in the amusement."

"Oh, pray, forgive me." Aunt's hand quivered and she spilled her tea.

He lifted an open hand. "Give it not second thought. I consider it a compliment when anyone forgets my deformity long enough to ask such a question."

Mary bit her lip. No matter how curious, there were questions one did not ask.

He met her eyes and nodded just a bit. "I have always used a cane. I was born with an odd ankle, you see. Left me unfit for farming or soldiering."

"Good thing you were given the mind for studying lest you were good for nothing at all." Mr. Lacey elbowed Mr. Parris and laughed.

Though Mr. Parris laughed too, a slight shadow around his eyes suggested that joke had been told too many times. Rather like some of Lydia's remarks.

"And let us not forget, you were an excellent tutor to all the young ladies in the house. They came direct to you for help learning their sums. As I recall, you proved far more patient than Mother when she taught them." Mr. Lacey swallowed a rather large gulp of tea. "I swear you have the patience of Job."

"Such flattery—do you not fear that I will fall to pride for it?"

Aunt and Uncle smiled and guffawed.

Mary licked her lips. "I have four sisters, two elder and two younger. I well understand challenges of having so many young women under the same roof."

"Five girls and no brothers?" Mr. Lacey's brows rose high.

"No brothers, just my poor father who spent many hours sequestered in his book room."

"At least, we had three boys in the house to keep my father in masculine companionship," Mr. Lacey said.

"There were eight of you?" Mary asked.

"Plus my aunt—Parris' mother—my grandparents and my father's uncle, fourteen of us all told. Made for some very merry times." One side of his lips turned up in a dimpled smile. "I do have a fondness for a very full house. There is always some entertainment to be had. Take Parris, he is a very entertaining fellow. When not playing, he reads very well."

Mr. Parris raked his hair back and shifted in his seat.

"What do you prefer to read?" Mary glanced at the bookcase.

Mr. Lacey hid a snort in his cup of tea.

It was the polite thing to ask, was it not? Or perhaps Mr. Lacey had been sarcastic in his remark. Sarcasm was so difficult to discern. She was forever misunderstanding Papa for it.

Mr. Parris did not appear to notice Mr. Lacey's amusement or her discomfort. He seemed very good at ignoring what he should not see. "Many things, histories, philosophy, even sermons. But I find company is most pleased by novels and poetry."

"Oh, it has been quite some time since I have heard poetry read. Do read us some." Aunt Philips hurried to the shelves and removed a book.

Mr. Parris turned the volume over in his hands and rifled through the pages. "This is quite familiar, *The Lady of the Lake*."

Mary bit her tongue. Though not awful, it was definitely not her first choice. She should not critique it yet. Perhaps after he read a passage, they might discuss its merits.

As he read, his voice deepened to a rhythmic, sonorous timbre filling the room and wrapping its occupants in a mesmerizing grip. His words painted mood and image with rare vibrancy.

Mary's spine tingled. How well he voiced King James and the bard, Allan Bane. How did he manage to change his tone so subtly, making each different, but not jarringly so? Eyes closed, she savored each word only to suffer aching loss when he stopped at the end of the first Canto. No matter how little she liked the poetry, she could hardly mention it after such a performance.

"That was extraordinary, Parris." Uncle blinked hard. "Shame you did not become a barrister. Oratory suits you."

"Would have made an excellent clergyman too," Mr. Lacey said.

"It was a tempting thought." Mr. Parris closed the book and set it aside. "I should have liked to be one."

Aunt poured a fresh cup of tea.

"What stopped you?" Mary added a bit of honey to soothe Mr. Parris' throat and handed it to him.

He sipped it. A small smile lifted the corner of his lips and he raised the teacup toward her with a small nod. "One does not always have the privilege of following one's dreams. In truth, it was a matter of practical consideration. You know there are far more curates than livings to be had. It is far commoner for a poor curate to remain a poor curate than to become a comfortable vicar. With no connections to vacant livings, and two sisters who might one day require my support, I felt it my duty to choose a more practical path."

"You are far too noble, and far too serious. We are gathered for amusement, not philosophical reflection," Mr. Lacey said.

"A hand of cards perhaps?" Aunt rose, "Or perhaps a board game? I know those to be a favorite among young people."

"Just the thing." Mr. Lacey joined her at the chest in the corner of the room, "That one looks like great fun."

Aunt cleared away the tea things and Uncle settled into his favorite chair with his newspaper.

Mr. Lacey set up the game while Mr. Parris read the rules aloud.

"Will you make the opening move, Miss Bennet?" Mr. Lacey handed her the dice.

Mary rolled, moved her piece and leaned back in her seat. What a welcome respite from the demands of conversation.

How intriguing the competition between the two men, more like brothers than cousins it seemed. Mr. Lacey was certainly the boldest, but Mr. Parris matched his brash moves with careful strategy.

"Ah, Miss Bennet, I fear the dice are against you this night. By rights, I may remove you from your leading potion and return you back from whence you came." Mr. Lacey's hand hovered over her game marker.

Mary sighed. Lydia took great pleasure in doing that very thing. Hopefully, he would not exult over it as she did. "It is part of the game. I believe one should not play unless they expect such adversity."

"True enough, but lacking gallantry all the same. I shall forgo the opportunity and take the less favorable path instead."

There was that sparkling-eyed smile once again, the one that spurred the flutter in her heart and a quickness in her breath.

Mr. Parris threw the dice.

"What ho!" Mr. Lacey leaned back in his chair.

"Chance is truly my adversary tonight!" Mary cried.

"Now you are faced with the same choice! I am keen to see what you will choose. Send Miss Bennet back a dozen spaces or choose the longer path as I did?"

Mr. Parris gazed at her. "Though it sets me up for ill comparison to you, I am not afraid to set the lady back a handful of spaces. I believe she will still achieve victory over us all, made sweeter knowing it was earned honestly." He slid her piece backward.

The lift of his eyebrow seemed more a challenge to rise to the occasion than a gloat of triumph.

As he predicted, she did win. The victory was difficult to savor amidst the confusing tension roiling in her belly. Even more unsettling, both young men insisted on paying her forfeits, kissing her cheeks under Aunt's steady gaze.

⚘Chapter 2

MARY SLEPT RESTLESSLY and rose early. Strange lingering dreams left her too restive for sewing and made reading a veritable impossibility. Perhaps writing might pass the time in useful effort. How fortunate that the sun in the morning room was ideal for the task.

"A letter to your mother?"

Mary jumped and nearly spoiled the final word of her sentence. "Oh, Aunt! Yes, yes, I am writing to her. It has been a week since my last correspondence."

"Well, do not mention your dinner with Mr. Lacey, not yet." Aunt Philips set her workbasket on the table.

"Why would I? We have only just met."

"It was a propitious meeting. You must agree."

"It was a pleasant evening." Mary sealed her ink bottle and sprinkled sand over her letter.

"Indeed it was, and you must make the most of it. We must act quickly, if you are to secure Mr. Lacey."

"Secure him? Is he a piece of livestock to be acquired like a cow or donkey."

"Do not be impertinent, young lady. You know very well what I mean."

"But I hardly know him."

"What has that to do with anything? We have seen he is agreeable enough and interested in you." Aunt snatched a bit of mending from her basket.

"He was being polite."

"I saw the way he looked at you. Polite is rarely that appreciative. I knew your sisters' gowns would turn the trick. Why must you be so stubborn?" Aunt stabbed the torn shirt with her needle. "Nevertheless, do not tell your mother just yet. You know how delicate her nerves are. She might become unnecessarily excited and hasten back to Meryton, leaving poor Kitty unattended."

"I had no intention of telling Mama anything." And after a threat like that, she would make a point never, ever to mention young men in any of her letters.

"I expect we shall see Mr. Lacey here quite regularly. I invited him to dine with us every Monday night until he has a cook and housekeeper."

"That was very kind of you, but what of Mr. Parris?"

"He may not be a match for you, but that does not mean I intend to be uncivil. He is included in the invitation as well. Mind you, I noticed his attentions to you, but do not worry over slighting his feeling. Surely, he must know he is nothing to his cousin."

"He was not flirting with me." Mary braced her forehead in her hand. "Neither of them were."

"Do not fret, child. Trust me to know what I am about. But, enough of that for now. I need your help to go marketing today. Do be a dear and help me with my list."

Try as she might to set the notion aside, Aunt's words echoed over and over in her mind. Had Mr. Lacey been particularly attentive to her or was his attention because she was the only young woman there? Had Mr. Parris been attending to her as well?

How did she feel if it were true?

How entirely and completely madding! When Jane and Lydia and Elizabeth were about, there was never any doubt as to the object of a young man's attention. No wonder the society of young men left Kitty twitterpated, wondering if this one or that one might like her.

Still, there was something warm and affirming in the possibility she might be liked, not merely settled for in the absence of her sisters. What would she do if she was?

Was it truly possible that she was as worthy of affection as her sisters?

There was only one way to know. She would accept Mr. Lacey's attentions. Perhaps he would prove a similar mind and compatible temperament, or at the very least, a tolerable one.

After two more dinners in the company of Mr. Lacey, the upcoming Midsummer's Day ball looked more appealing than any such event ever had. How would it be, being like every other girl, caring about her dress, her hair, anticipating dancing with a desirable partner? It was almost too much to consider.

Lizzy's white ball gown suddenly became far more interesting than any other dress ever had. For the first time in her life, a trip to the haberdasher proved absolutely essential. She stole a last look at the dress, picked up her reticule and bonnet and trotted down the stairs.

Aunt met her in the front hall. "Mary, dear, Miss Grant has taken ill. I must call upon her and bring her my special tonic. It always sets her to rights. I cannot go with you to the haberdasher today."

Mary clutched the banister tightly. "Of course, I understand." The dress did not truly need to be embellished. She would bear the privation with equanimity easily enough, experienced as she was in brooking disappointment.

"We shall go tomorrow."

"Have you not promised to take the morning with Mrs. King and the afternoon with Mrs. Goulding?"

Aunt Philips threw her head back and huffed. "How can I be so forgetful? Such things never used to slip my mind. I suppose worrying about the welfare of a young lady has made me much like your mother. She would think it quite the jolly jape to see me so addlepated now."

Uncle peeked out of his office. "I believe I may have a solution to your little hubble-bubble." He strode out to them, looking excessively proud of himself.

"What would that be?" Aunt leaned back and cocked her head.

"I must send Mr. Parris to the stationers. One cannot run a law office without quills and paper, you know. I will ask him to accompany you on your errands."

"That is an excellent idea. What do you think, Mary?"

"Young Millie can go with me. I am certain Cook can spare her from the kitchen."

"No, I need her to attend Mrs. Grant with me. I have two large baskets and cannot manage them both myself."

"Parris will be going out, with or without you and the haberdasher is on his way. It is not as if you will be interfering with his work."

Mary wrung her hands. Going out was never so difficult when she had a house full of sisters for company. "As long as it will not be an imposition on either of you."

"Think nothing of it. I am pleased to be able to assist my ladies."

"With so little trouble to yourself." Aunt wagged a finger at him.

Uncle waved her off. "I shall go and inform Mr. Parris."

A quarter of an hour later, Mr. Parris met her at the front door.

"So which cane do you carry today, sir?" she asked, glancing toward his left hand.

"I do not believe you have seen this one before." He held the cane handle out to her.

"Oh, is that, yes, it is, a cat. Out of ivory?" She stroked the dear little head between the ears. Some very clever craftsman had even carved tabby stripes along its back.

"Nothing so elegant, it is fashioned from hart's horn. Do you like it?"

"Far better than the wooden knob painted with insects." She handed it back to him and shuddered.

He laughed. "I confess, my sisters quite dislike that one as well. When I was a younger man, I did on occasion torment them with it."

"I can easily see how you might. How came you by such a … unique object?"

"It is something of a joke in my family you see, to find the most outlandish handles for my walking stick. That one in particular was a gift from Lacey. He has given me a few others, which must not be brought out in polite company."

"And you do not mind?"

"Heavens, no! I find it much easier to accept my condition and make light of it when I can. How dreary to bemoan the act of Providence that made me what I am. Who would want to keep company with me then? Others are far more at ease with me knowing it is safe to speak aloud what politeness might only allow them to whisper." He opened the door for her and they set off.

"Your philosophy is most extraordinary, sir."

"It has served me well. Would you care for company at the haberdashers? As I recall, young ladies generally prefer to obtain the opinions of others before settling their own minds regarding the trims for their gowns."

"You seem to know young ladies well, but does your expertise extend to ribbons and lace?" She caught his gaze with a sidelong glance.

"And muslins, silks and calicos as well. With two sisters and three cousins, I often found myself called upon as an arbiter of good taste." His expression was all openness and sincerity.

"And you accepted such a role willingly? When lace was mentioned at Longbourn, my father would turn his back and stalk off crying 'No lace, madam, no lace!'"

Mr. Parris stepped carefully around a rut in the road. "My uncle felt much the same way—and Lacey too, for that matter. Despite all his excellent qualities, the appreciation of fine textiles is not among them."

"If you are sanguine on the matter, I should appreciate your input." If nothing else, it should be an interesting exercise to compare his comments to what Lydia and Kitty would typically offer.

He opened the shop door for her and bowed her in.

"Ah, Miss Bennet," the haberdasher hurried toward her. "It is so good to see you. I have not seen any of your family in quite some time. I despaired some great offense might have been committed."

"With Lydia's marriage and Kitty's travel with our parents, there is far less call for lace at Longbourn. But I come now for trimmings for a ball gown."

"A ball gown—for you, Miss?"

Mary blushed and turned away from Mr. Parris' inquiring gaze.

"What had you in mind?"

"I…I…do not quite know. I wish to trim the skirt of a white muslin gown."

The haberdasher turned aside, but she could still make out the mild annoyance in his eyes. "Flounces along the bottom of a gown are very popular with young ladies right now. I have suggested several for the upcoming Midsummer ball. Let me show you." He shuffled to an overstuffed shelf and returned with several laces and trims: ruched ribbon, padded ribbon, braids and bobbles. "They often take several of these in rows following the bottom hem of the skirt. Very fashionable."

Mary rubbed her fingertips along her lips. "Those are very nice. Perhaps the white satin. How many rows would you suggest?"

"I would say three, perhaps alternated with the ruched ribbon and perhaps a lace." He held up his hand and leaned in to whisper behind it. "I have good reason to believe Miss Michaelson and Miss King both plan to use such decorations on their gowns."

She chewed her knuckles and shook her head. "I am hesitant to copy designs used by others. It seems a sure way to breed animosity. Perhaps I ought to leave the gown as it is. It may suit me best left unadorned."

"If I might suggest?" Mr. Parris leaned on the haberdasher's counter. "Perhaps this silk ribbon gathered and fixed on a skirt as if a garland. Bows and perhaps a cluster of ribbon rosettes cradled in the curve of the crescents would make for a unique decoration."

The haberdasher's eyebrows danced on his forehead. He rushed to a drawer, then two more and returned with arms laden. He laid down a piece of muslin on the counter. "Now what you describe might be achieved thusly." He laid several lengths of ribbon along the muslin. A shapely crescent formed. He added very pale pink bows and rosettes.

"I think I should like it better without the bows, just the rosettes."

The haberdasher removed the bows.

"Yes, like that." She glanced up at Mr. Parris.

"I will convey your compliments to my sister. She arranged one of her own skirts very much like this. She is of a similar disposition to yourself, so I thought you would find it equally pleasing."

"Shall I deliver these to Longbourn?"

"No, to the Philips'; I am staying there."

"Very well, miss. You shall have it later today." He bowed and scurried away off.

Mr. Parris offered his arm.

She hesitated.

"It is safe, fear not."

She blushed and laid her fingers on his forearm. "Excuse me…"

"Not at all. I am complimented you would take my arm at all."

They stepped outside.

"Shall I escort you back to your uncle's house now, or shall we attend to the stationer's first?"

His smile was rather charming and she was low on ink and a new quill would be nice. "I should like to go to the stationer's."

"My pleasure, Miss Bennet."

A large, shadowy blur approached from her left.

"Parris! Miss Bennet! Capital to see you this morning."

"Lacey, what are you doing here?" Parris released her and stepped slightly away.

"Business, always business, you know that. Just finished one meeting at the pub. Taking a bit of fresh air before going in for another. And you? I thought a clerk never saw the sun when on his master's time."

"That is often true, but Miss Bennet required an escort today. The duty fell to me as I am out to procure the stock of our trade, pen and paper."

"Where would a young lady like you go on such a lovely day? The confectioner perhaps? I wonder what your favorite sweet might be. Marzipan?"

She hated marzipan, but there was no need to mention that. "We called at the haberdasher's."

"Ah, the bane of men everywhere. Did Parris offer his informed opinions of the fripperies?"

"I welcomed his advice."

"As did my sisters. You should have been a tailor or mantua maker."

Mr. Parris cocked his head. "Perhaps I have missed my calling."

"Why do I not walk Miss Bennet home? No need to bother her with your paper and quills."

"I am sure she will find that agreeable." Mr. Parris bowed from his shoulders and backed away.

Mr. Lacey offered his arm. "I am very happy to be of service, madam."

"Good day, then." Mr. Parris hobbled away with his odd grasshopper gait.

They strolled toward the Phillips' house.

"He is a good soul, Parris is, even if he can be a bit dry and dull."

"He has an excellent eye for satin and lace."

Mr. Lacey laughed. "That he does—not the most manly of achievements, I fear, but it is one of his most notable."

"It makes you uncomfortable?"

"I would not say that so much as it limits the conversation. I am glad you found his company agreeable though."

"Mary, Mary, wait! Mr. Lacey…" Maria Lucas rushed up, panting.

"Is there something amiss?" Mary caught her elbow, lest she fall. "You should not exert yourself so."

"No…no…not at all, it is quite well. I am just so excited, I could not contain myself." Sweat trickled down the side of her flushed face.

"Do tell, Miss Lucas, why such excitement?" Mr. Lacey said.

"My mother has sent me on a most delightful errand. She wishes me to convey, to all of you, an invitation to dinner, at our house on Friday. The Gouldings and the Michaelsons have also been invited. Do say you shall be able to attend. I do so long for some fun company. You know how droll the Gouldings can be."

"I can speak for Parris and me. We have no engagements that day. You may convey our thanks to Lady Lucas."

"I do not believe we have any fixed appointments either. I will check with my aunt to be sure. I enjoy the Gouldings, though, and shall look forward to their society."

"Oh, Mary, do not be a scold—Lydia and Kitty agree with me and I know that you do, too." Maria folded her arms and huffed.

Her face lost color and she flung out her arms. Mary and Mr. Lacey caught her on either side.

"Oh, oh, I fear you were right. I should not have run about so. I am quite dizzy." Maria clutched Mr. Lacey's arm.

"We must get you home, Maria." Mary released her elbow.

"Yes, yes, I suppose so. Will you see me there, Mr. Lacey?" She looked up at him, batting her eyes.

"I would be happy to see you there, but..." He glanced at Mary.

"No, no, I shall be fine. It is only a short way to my Uncle's. Maria is in far greater need."

"You are certain?"

"Yes." Mary curtsied and hurried away.

Lydia was apt to abandon her when they went to town together. It would not be the first time she had walked a short way through town alone. She rushed past the stationers.

"Miss Bennet?"

Her feet countermanded her will and stopped in place.

Mr. Parris caught up to her. "Are you well? What happened?"

"To Mr. Lacey?" She quickly explained, face turned away from his inquisitive gazes.

"I see." Mr. Parris pressed his lips into several distinct frowns. "I am sorry. He does so like to be helpful but he sometimes becomes distracted."

"Truly it is of no—"

"Pray, Miss Bennet, do not feel the need to be so brave on my account. I well know the foibles of my cousin and feel the offense he has caused, even inadvertently."

"There is truly no need."

"Allow me to try and make up for his abandonment. I would be honored to complete the service I promised to render." He raised an eyebrow, cocked his head, and offered his arm.

"When you put it that way, I can hardly refuse." She slipped her hand in the crook of his elbow and adjusted herself to his peculiar gait. His arm was not as strong as Mr. Lacey's, to be sure, but there was something quite steady there despite his limp.

Chapter 3

"THOSE LUCASES ARE AN artful family." Aunt Philips tucked a final pin into Mary's hair.

The image staring back from her looking glass favored one of her sisters more than it did herself. Delicate ringlets surrounded her long face in uneasy competition with her very round glasses. She removed them, but the mirror blurred, and she could barely make out her image. Alas, there was no way around it. She must wear her glasses to dinner.

"I want you to be sure to pay every attention to Mr. Lacey tonight. Those Lucases, I am sure, have designs on him for Maria. Lizzy lost Mr. Collins to that plain, cunning Charlotte. I will not have you losing to another Lucas."

"Do you not think Lizzy's match with Mr. Darcy far more—"

"That is not the point. The issue is the Lucases and their over-high aspirations. It is not to be borne. My dear sister would surely say the same thing. So tonight, you shall put yourself forward to be witting and charming and lovely like your sisters. That way, Mr. Lacey shall not even notice that dreadful Maria Lucas."

"Maria is my friend."

"When in the marriage mart, my dear, a single woman cannot find true friends among other single women. The luxury of true friendship only comes after one is safely married."

"Or on the shelf." Mary muttered.

"What was that?"

"Maria is my friend. I will not suddenly consider her my enemy because young men have moved into the neighborhood."

"Not young men, an eligible young farmer who already has paid great attention to you. All I ask is you do not allow him to forget the preference he has already shown for you. Now then, those beads and ribbons look so fashionable in your hair. Who knew you might be every bit as pretty as—well not Jane or Lydia, but certainly Kitty and perhaps even Lizzy."

Mary forced a smile—the surest way to end such an appalling line of conversation.

"Come now, your uncle has brought the gig around. We must not be the last to arrive."

Mary followed Aunt Philips out.

Each time a surface caught her reflection, she started. Was allowing Aunt Philips to dress and arrange her hair a terrible mistake? Had it given her leave to demand Mary act in a way entirely unlike herself?

Could she do it—see those she had regarded as friends as dangerous rivals and even enemies?

No, that was not going to be.

It was one thing to take pleasure in a young man's attentions. But she could not allow it to influence her character. Either Mr. Lacey would like her for herself alone, or not at all.

That is what Lizzy insisted upon, and it served her well, did it not? Surely it was a sensible philosophy.

The ride to the Lucas's passed quickly. Traveling with just aunt and uncle always seemed so easy. Piling all her sisters, plus Mama and Papa in the coach inevitably took far longer. A sharp pang pinched her heart. That would never happen again, even once her family returned to Longbourn. She would never live with Jane, Lizzy and Lydia again.

Unless she had to rely on their charity as a poor spinster. Aunt Philips was trying to prevent that fate.

Great heavens, when did life become so complicated?

Lady Lucas met them at the door, the picture of graciousness and affected elegance. Only those who had seen true elegance like the Darcys' or the Gardiners', might call them affected, though. Mary certainly would not call attention to the issue.

The Gouldings had already arrived, as had Mr. Lacey and Mr. Parris, much to Aunt's dismay. In the drawing room, Miss Goulding and Maria sat near Mr. Lacey, apparently engrossed in one of his amusing tales. He had a vast number of them.

Mr. Parris talked with Sir William and Mr. Goulding, or rather; he seemed to listen very intently to Sir William who generally talked enough for three.

Mary hesitated at the door. Aunt's firm push between her shoulders propelled her, stumbling off balance, toward Mr. Lacey and his bevy of admirers.

"Miss Bennet." Mr. Lacey rose and bowed.

Maria and Miss Goulding followed suit, but neither appeared pleased to bring another young woman into the conversation.

"Pray take my seat." He held his chair for her and brought a chair from the other side of the room. He placed the Trafalgar chair just to Mary's left and sat.

He could have sat beside Mrs. Goulding. Perhaps Aunt Philips was correct.

"Do finish your tale, sir." Miss Goulding batted her eyes just like Lydia used to do.

"Perhaps another time. Miss Bennet has little interest in horse racing. I do not care to tax her good will."

"I would not be such fastidious a kill-joy," Miss Goulding murmured.

Mary's cheeks burned with the familiar sensation of censure. "Pray do not suspend Miss Goulding's pleasure on my account."

"Are you certain, Miss Bennet?"

Something in the way he looked at her, in his tone of voice left her insides all warm and fuzzy and soothed her raised hackles.

"Pray, continue your tale."

He launched into an animated description of a horse race that she promptly ceased to follow. While his consideration was most pleasing, he did appear quite satisfied to share his tale with Maria and Miss

Goulding. Soon Miss Michaelson joined them and hung off his every word. Perhaps she should feign greater interest. He did seem so pleased by his audience's rapt attention.

Lady Lucas took Sir William's arm and paraded to the doorway. "Dinner is served."

Mary stepped back to allow the married ladies to find their escorts. Master John Lucas claimed Miss Michaelson, who looked a bit disappointed. Maria and Miss Goulding cast expectant looks toward Mr. Lacey.

He was all gallantry, in the style of Beau Brummel, offering an arm to each of them. They giggled and accepted his offer.

Mary hung back further. Aunt would not be pleased. But, how could she endure the awkwardness of calling attention to her lack of an escort? She had walked into the Lucas's dining room alone enough times to know the way on her own.

"I fear you must resign yourself to walking with me again." Mr. Parris offered his arm. "Unless you prefer to walk unaccompanied, which I can accept without offence should you so desire."

She peered at his guileless expression. How could he be so gracious?

"I am honored to accompany you, sir."

They walked into the dining room. How much easier now to follow his odd gait than when she had walked with him only a few days ago.

Two places remained at the dining table by the time they arrived, neither near Mr. Lacey. She sat between Mrs. Goulding and Mr. Parris. As usual, Mrs. Goulding had little interest in her. Happily, Mr. Parris was content to engage her in conversation.

He offered astute observations upon the sermon the vicar had read the preceding week. More notably, he actually sought her opinion and listened to her answer carefully enough to question her on it.

Her rebuttal was interrupted by Lady Lucas rising from her seat. "Shall we adjourn, ladies?"

Usually the ladies' withdrawal was a relief from the dining room's stilted conversation, but tonight she felt the loss. Perhaps she might continue her discussion with Mr. Parris when the men joined them in the drawing room.

At least, Aunt would be pleased that their withdrawal would remove Mr. Lacey from Miss Goulding's and Maria's attentions.

Instead of walking with the married women, Aunt Philips hung back and caught Mary by the elbow. "You see it is exactly as I told you. Artful! How neatly you were separated from Mr. Lacey for the whole of the evening."

"He was merely being gracious to—"

"That may be the case, but do not allow his good nature to be used against you. Make sure you sit near him when the men join us. And do not offer to play tonight—of course, you must do so if asked, though. I fear those sly girls will use your vanity about your playing to separate you from him. We must not permit that."

Mary screwed her eyes shut. Yes, her misplaced vanity. Would she never live that down? At least the injunction not to play was a welcome one.

Aunt Philips squeezed her wrist hard. "Did you hear me girl? Or are you off wool gathering as Lizzy was apt to do?"

"No, I was attending you, Aunt. I just thought—"

"This is not the time for you to think. Just listen to me. Do not go on, headstrong and opinionated as she. She gave your mother no end of grief."

"Yet she married such a man as Mr. Darcy," Mary muttered.

"And how that was accomplished one might never fathom. She certainly did nothing to deserve it," Aunt grumbled under her breath. "It does not do you well to compare yourself to Lizzy, you know. You have not her assets in your favor. She is prettier than you and far more pleasing company. Do not take this opportunity lightly. You might not have another." She stopped them both just outside the drawing room. "What do you want for your life, Mary? You are not yet on the shelf, but not far from it. Do you truly want to be the maiden aunt passed from household to household with nothing but your trunk to call your own?"

"This is not—"

"Yes, it is. Charlotte barely escaped that fate and at your expense."

Mary's face flushed.

"Your mother may have ignored it, but I saw how you hoped for Mr. Collins' attentions. He would have been an excellent match for you, and you a sensible wife to him, not to mention you are far prettier than *she.*"

Mary looked away, blinking hard.

"You see, I am right. I do not wish to see that happen to you again, especially not with one of her sisters."

No one knew the depth of disappointment she had suffered. To have it brought up now—this was too cruel.

"It is clear you agree with me. So, do not sit idly by and allow another girl to take what should be yours." She brushed past Mary and into the drawing room. "Lady Lucas, what a lovely meal."

How could one hate a truth so much, yet it be correct? She had not seen Charlotte's machinations for what they were. Lizzy was her particular friend. It was right for Charlotte to give way to Lizzy's prior claim. But Mary had no such privilege. The hurt of Charlotte's actions ran deeper than was safe to admit.

Now, Mr. Lacey was here, and she liked him. Moreover, he paid her particular attentions. Even Mr. Parris seemed to agree, and promoted his cousin's suit. What foolishness to throw that away simply by not behaving as other girls did?

She would conquer this reticence somehow. With squared shoulders, she strode into the drawing room.

Her resolve, though pleasing to Aunt Philips, accomplished little that night. Mr. Lacey and Mr. Parris never made it to the drawing room after dinner.

A stable boy had arrived with word of a sick horse—a favorite horse—and Mr. Lacey left directly to attend it. Without another way home, Mr. Paris had little option but to depart with his cousin. After all, he certainly could not walk the whole distance back to the Oliver farm.

Dejected, Maria gave up the notion of parlor games, sinking into a most ill-suited melancholy. Lady Lucas insisted on cards. After only a few hands though, everyone lost interest and wandered away to small conversation clusters, none of which included Mary.

She welcomed a few moments to herself for reflection and settled herself near the bookshelf. It was a shame to lose the possibility of continuing her conversation with Mr. Parris.

But perhaps it was best this way. How difficult it would have been to endure Maria, Miss Goulding and Miss Michaelson fawning over Mr. Lacey as she struggled to hold her own in that company. Even if he was merely polite, most of Mr. Lacey's attentions would have been fixed upon other girls leaving her tempted to jealousy—a far too familiar vice.

Aunt Philips kept her opinions to herself until they squashed into the gig, but not one moment more.

"It was greatly to your favor that Mr. Lacey left as early as he did." She plucked at her skirt.

"I am surprised you say that."

"Did you not see how attentive John Lucas and young Michaelson became to the other girls? I even heard them claiming dances for the ball. Mr. Lacey has already claimed a dance with you. I believe those little chits will feel that quite keenly."

"They are not chits, and I have no wish to make them feel badly."

"That may be so, but it does not change the fact that you are already set to dance with him and they are not. I am most satisfied."

Chapter 4

A FORTNIGHT LATER, Mary climbed onto Uncle Philips' gig once more. She bit her lip and swallowed back the butterflies dancing in her stomach. The gig's tight quarters prevented her from fidgeting, which all things considered, was probably good. It would not do to muss her lovely gown.

Despite being Lizzy's old frock, it was the most beautiful thing she had ever owned. Embellished as it was—to Mr. Parris's suggestions—it was stunning, perhaps even too fine for a plain face and figure like hers. Still, it was very pleasing to be dressed as prettily as the rest of the girls in the room, even if she could never be as appealing.

Jealousy was a most unbecoming emotion and a difficult voice to quell. It grew even louder watching true beauties like Miss Michaelson and Miss Goulding saunter past, on the arms of their first partners.

The ballroom blazed with candles, reflecting off mirrors on every wall. Roses-filled vases and bowls on every surface suffused the air with the perfume of summer. She closed her eyes and drew in a deep breath. Such fragrance deserved to be savored.

Aunt Philips nudged her—in truth it was more of a shove—toward a knot of other young ladies. Every instinct demanded she find a corner to hide in or a pianoforte at which to be useful. But she must not. Tonight, she was to seek partners, dance and socialize—particularly with Mr. Lacey.

Oh! Oh! There he was, with Mr. Parris in his shadow. How dapper they looked, both of them. Mr. Lacey cut a fine figure in his buckskin breeches. Skin tight, they accented his excellent legs and easy, elegant movement. His close-cut coat defined his broad shoulders and powerful chest held erect with perfect posture. She averted her eyes—she must not stare.

Mr. Parris preferred simple trousers. He had confided to her that though far less elegant, he believed they increased the comfort of those around him, hiding his disfigurement.

He was so considerate.

Her cheeks flushed as they drew near and her glasses slipped down her nose. She shoved them up into place. Had she only been able to leave them at home. But her best efforts were entirely thwarted by the weakness of her eyes.

"Good evening, ladies." Mr. Lacey bowed.

Mr. Parris shadowed him.

The girls beside her tittered, just as Kitty and Lydia would have.

Mary curtsied. "Good evening."

"Have you a partner already for the first dance, Miss Bennet?"

Jealous glances buffeted her from both sides. "No, sir, I do not."

"Then might I have the honor of the first dance with you?"

"Y-yes, thank you."

Pray, let the dance be something she knew well!

The musicians played a few notes. She took his arm, and he led her to the gaily chalked dance floor. What a shame those celestial images and sailing ships would suffer under their dancing slippers, disappearing as the night progressed.

As she passed Mr. Parris, he tipped his head and smiled. Something about his posture lent an air of sadness to his countenance. Perhaps she might be able to inquire after that later.

"Forgive me, I have not been here long enough to know where to stand," he whispered.

Her cheeks burned. Where was her rank in this group? She chewed her lip and squeezed her eyes shut. Where had Jane and Lizzy stood when they danced? Several couples above Charlotte and Maria.

She opened her eyes and inclined her head. "There."

How peculiar it felt, proceeding toward the top of the set—odd and uncomfortable. What if she made a misstep or tripped? Though she never had before, Lydia would declare it just her luck to do so now.

"Is it not exhilarating to see so many couples on the dance floor?" Mr. Lacey gazed up and down the set.

"My sisters found it so."

"You do not like to dance?"

"With two elder sisters and two, far livelier, younger ones, I found I did not often have the opportunity."

"Well, then it must be made up for now."

Miss Michaelson strode to the top of the room and announced, "Dover Pier."

The musicians began the lively, lilting tune.

Thank heavens! Jane and Kitty liked this tune so well that they had often danced it at home.

"You approve the dance then?" His lips drifted up into a charming smile, one Lydia would have waxed on about for days.

"It is most agreeable."

He extended his arm and took her gloved hand in his. How very large and strong his hands were. Kitty had been apt to note a man's hands. Now it made sense.

"Are cotillions popular here?"

"Mrs. Michaelson prefers to have them played during the second half of the evening, after supper restores the dancers a bit. On occasion, she has even included a reel among the sets."

"A reel? I shall look forward to that. I believe those are my favorite dances."

Somehow that seemed entirely right and fitting. The gaiety of the reel fit him very well. Best not share her own opinion of that dance, though. He might take it as a criticism of himself.

She nearly lost count on their two-hand turn. Once and a half around was difficult to keep track of. But he cleverly covered her misstep and did not appear to notice.

Surely though, some of the ladies observed it and would be sniggering about it later, behind their fans.

Once at the bottom of the set, they stood silent, catching their breath for several minutes.

"I say, Meryton abounds with excellent dancers," he said, gaze fixed on the couple turning by the right hands beside them.

"Mary King is only recently returned to Meryton. She has long been acknowledged an excellent dancer among us."

"That is good to hear for Michaelson pressed me to engage her for the second dance tonight."

The pinch in her chest reminded her of the familiar ache that would no doubt open up again. It always plagued her when she sat alone, along the walls, and watched the dancers form up for a set she would not dance.

Heavens!

She must cease such useless thoughts. He had asked her for this dance and had to be encouraged toward asking Mary King. Moreover, there was no good reason to believe she might not be asked to dance again tonight. There seemed plenty of partners to go around. Mrs. Michaelson planned her guest list well. Mr. Lacey might even ask her a second time. If Aunt Philips was correct, such a thing could indeed happen.

"I dare say you will enjoy a number of excellent partners tonight. This is your first ball among us, and your company will be most sought after," she said.

"One of the advantages of being new to a neighborhood, I suppose. But when word spreads that I am apt to trod upon toes and hems, my popularity will suffer most cruelly." He turned his smile and twinkling eyes on her.

Bubbling effervescence rose within, fueling a smile she could not suppress.

"Forgive me for being so forward, but that is a most pleasing expression."

A blush began at her shoulders and raced from her cheeks to her hair line.

"You are not accustomed to compliments? No need to answer. I see that I am right. It is such a shame, though. Every woman should enjoy her share of them."

The music ended, and he escorted her from the dance floor.

"Thank you for the pleasure of the dance." He bowed.

She blinked, and he was gone—doubtlessly looking for his next partner. Though being alone in a crowd was her most common state, tonight it took on an unfamiliar poignancy. Mr. Lacey's company always ran bitter sweet—sweet whilst it lasted, but bitter in its brevity.

Was it selfish to prefer greater constancy from a gentleman?

Tap-shuffle-step-tap-shuffle-step

Mr. Parris?

She turned.

"I thought you might appreciate a glass of punch after your dance." He offered her a cup but had not one for himself.

Oh, of course! He could not possibly carry two at once with his cane. How thoughtful.

"Thank you, I am a bit parched." She took the cup from him, his gloved fingers brushing hers.

Did they linger just a bit?

"Have you a partner for the next?"

"Not at present."

"May I assist in finding you one? Since I cannot execute the office myself, the least I can do is to find a suitable substitute in my place."

Her breath hitched. "Thank you for the offer, but I should like to sit out for this one. I must catch my second wind." Was he trying to rid himself of her company already?

His eyes brightened, and he stood a little straighter. "Are you fatigued? Shall we find a place to sit?"

"I…yes that would be quite pleasant."

He guided her to a bench stationed against a brightly painted screen dividing the dancers from a narrow walk way to the dining room.

"I had not noticed this spot." She scooted to one side to give him room to sit as well.

"I am quite accomplished at finding out of the way places to sit." A wry smiled turned up the corners of his mouth.

How uniquely charming his easy humility.

"Perhaps that is an accomplishment we both share." She sipped her punch.

Oh, it was particularly strong tonight. Best not drink it too quickly.

"So have you finished the sermon I recommended?" he asked.

"I have indeed."

"How did you find it related to that sermon of Fordyce—"

"It was a most remarkable illustration—"

"Of his third and fifth points?" He cocked his head, eyebrows rising on the question.

How agreeable it was to have one's conversation partner so attentive as to anticipate her comments.

"Exactly. One might easily wonder if the author had that purpose in mind upon writing it."

"Oh!" Dancers jostled the screen.

"I say, are you all right, Martin?" That was Mr. Lacey's voice behind the screen. "Or have you already had too much punch."

"Who put a ruddy screen up in the midst of a dance floor?"

"Good thing the ladies are all dancing together this measure. Neither of our partners would be apt to forgive such a clumsy move."

"Indeed, Miss Michaelson," Mr. Martin's tone rose an octave, "has little tolerance for inelegant partners."

Mr. Lacey snickered.

"Do not be so quick to laugh. Miss King has equally high standards. I am sure your first partner did you no favors in preparing you for her"

"Miss Bennet?"

"Indeed she is an indifferent dancer I would say."

Mary flushed. She had only danced once with Mr. Martin and it had been a miserably memorable affair. He had trod on her toes and ruined her slippers.

"You are too harsh."

"Perhaps you are right. She is better than indifferent, but still nothing compared to Miss King."

How kind of Mr. Martin to allow that.

"I grant you that. But she is a very pleasant, comfortable sort of girl."

Pleasant and comfortable were not so bad were they?

"Are such charms worth spectacles and but fifty pounds a year? Consider, you are dancing with an heiress of considerable fortune," Mr. Martin said.

"I cannot see her family approving—"

"You might be surprised. I heard her brothers talking. Ten thousand pounds is a temptation to many men and yet she returned unengaged. Her manners, it seems, were not polished enough for her London season to be wholly successful."

"That bad?"

"It has been said…Consider, you are on your way to becoming a properly landed gentleman. If you can make her like you, you have a very good chance at receiving the family's approbation. I do not think they relish facing the *ton* again."

"That is an interesting notion," Mr. Lacey said.

"Are not freckles and a fortune much more appealing than a merely comfortable woman with so much less?"

"When you put it that way—yes, Miss King is a most lovely partner. Very worth pleasing."

Mary sprang to her feet and rushed away.

Air! She needed air most desperately. How could anyone breathe with so very many people milling about?

A pair of partially open French doors led to a small balcony obscured by curtains. Well out of the way, she might spend the rest of the evening here.

What choice had she? How might she face any of them again?

An indifferent dancer—no a tolerable one, better that was. True, she would never be a picture of grace like Jane, but was she truly such a trial to stand up with?

She removed her glasses and blotted her cheeks with her handkerchief. At least she had been deemed pleasant, oh yes, that and comfortable. Two very high compliments indeed. Neither attribute made up for a lack of fortune. Nor did her 'beauty', marred as it was by her spectacles, do anything to atone for her relative poverty. She sniffled and bit her knuckle. How foolish to believe a man might like her well enough to overlook—

"Miss Bennet?"

She jumped and turned. Mr. Parris stood in the doorway, an elegant shadow backlit by glittering candlelight from the ballroom.

"I shall not ask if you are well for any fool could discern that you are not. Is there anything I might do for your relief?"

She turned away and clutched the iron railing. "Thank you, sir but I can think of nothing."

He moved closer, his shoulder almost touching hers. "It is never pleasant to hear oneself spoken of."

"Unless you have great fortune or beauty."

"Or charm, I dare say. I have heard my cousins spoken of much as you have your sisters."

"I know no one else who understands."

"It is not something I would wish upon anyone." He leaned heavily against the railing.

"No, it is not."

"I suppose when one has many admirable qualities one dares set their sights very high. But it leaves that one apt to miss virtues less quantifiable."

She turned just enough to see his face from the corner of her eye. His sympathy and the moonlight made a handsome combination.

"Kind heartedness and consideration, faithfulness and a pleasing temper, all seasoned with thoughtful conversation and a liberal measure of like-mindedness are heavy inducements to any man of sense."

Her breath hitched and caught in her throat.

"Forgive me. I have spoken far too freely. I forget myself." He bowed and left her alone on the balcony.

She blinked and swallowed hard as she followed his retreat with her gaze.

Why could more men not be like him? Why could Mr. Lacey not be? How unfair for one man to have all the charm and fortune and the other all the character.

Beastly unfair.

A chill settled between her shoulders and worked its way toward her heart. Why had she dared let down her guard tonight?

Mr. Parris's shadow reappeared. He peeked into the balcony. "Miss Bennet, I pray you will come. It is a matter of some urgency."

No words offered themselves available for her use, so she merely nodded and followed him inside.

They wove through crowded rooms and stopped in a quiet corner near the retiring rooms. Mr. Lacey stood, staring at the floor, scuffing his toes along the floorboards.

"What?" Mary whispered trying to catch Mr. Parris's gaze.

He assiduously avoided her and gestured toward his cousin. "I believe Lacey has something to say to you." He stepped back, out of sight.

"Miss Bennet," Mr. Lacey rubbed the back of his neck. "I am given to understand you had the misfortune of hearing a most unguarded conversation."

"Be assured it was not my intention to invade upon your privacy."

"It was a very stupid thing for me to say—"

He tried to meet her gaze, but she deftly avoided him.

"Ill-advised altogether. I gravely insulted you."

She shrugged. "Merely reminded me of the realities of the world. One must be attentive to the issues of status and fortune."

"Pray, Miss Bennet, do not put words in my mouth."

"I did not put them there. I believe you did."

He winced and turned aside.

Aunt Philips would not be pleased with her boldness.

"Will you not permit me to apologize?" His voice took on an almost pleading note.

"Only if it is honestly meant, not an affectation of propriety." She glanced away.

Mr. Parris stood two paces away, focused on the painting that hung on the wall behind them. No doubt he could hear everything. At first glance, his expression was impassive, but beneath that he wore an air of noble sacrifice.

Mr. Lacey bowed. "I am most heartily sorry for my thoughtless, unfeeling words. I spoke without thinking, as one does in the casual company of those who pay little attention to what is said."

Perhaps he understood…

"I deeply regret any discomfort I have brought you."

Discomfort, was that what he would deem the sick knot in her belly—one that would form every time she was in society for the rest of this year, and perhaps longer?

Mr. Parris winced.

He understood.

"I regret you witnessed so great a lapse in my judgment. It was most ungentlemanly of me. I regret injuring your sensibilities."

Mr. Parris squeezed his eyes shut. He recognized sharp words slice to the core. More than mere sensibilities were injured.

If only Mr. Lacey could be more like Mr. Parris.

She turned to look at Mr. Parris more directly.

Mr. Lacey edged a little closer. "I should like it very much if you would dance the next with me."

Mr. Parris' jaw twitched. Mr. Lacey might like it, but Mr. Parris, it seemed did not.

A wave of warmth washed over her.

Gracious goodness! Mr. Parris?

"Miss Bennet?"

"I…" She turned back to Mr. Lacey. "I thank you for your offer, sir, but I shall not dance this set."

He started, eyes wide.

Had he never been turned down for a dance before?

"Oh, perhaps then the supper set?"

"Thank you, but no. I believe I shall not dance again tonight." She stood a little straighter.

Aunt Philips would have some very strong words to say of this. And Mary would listen politely. Yet the soaring sense of freedom that threatened to carry her off into the night could not lie. This was what she wanted, and it was right.

Mr. Lacey's face fell and his shoulders slumped a little. "I did not mean to steal away your pleasure this evening."

"I rarely dance. As Mr. Martin observed, I am ill-practiced and my performance is not a pleasing one. It is best for everyone this way. I shall not hold it against you to find yourself another partner." She curtsied.

"You are most gracious, Miss Bennet." He bowed and strode away, glancing over his shoulder at Mr. Parris as he went.

Would Mr. Lacey consider this a set-down, or was it a reprieve from an unpleasant sentence?

Mr. Parris closed the distance between them.

"Why did you do that?" Mary asked.

"Though he might occasionally be…thoughtless… that is not his nature. He is not cruel. I know he would want to make the situation right."

"His apology was very pretty."

"Why did you not accept his invitation to dance? You would give up your entire evening to make a point to him?"

"Because…" She met his gaze full on. "Do you truly wish I had?"

His face flushed and he stammered.

"Then why bring him to me?"

"His prospects are much greater than my own."

"And Mary King has far more to offer than I."

"So we both defer to beauty and fortune?" He shrugged.

"I suppose it is a habit of a lifetime."

"I fear I am about to speak too much. But a word or gesture from you will stop me." He studied her.

His stare, every bit as intense as Mr. Darcy's when he gaped at Elizabeth, held her fixed, nearly unable to breathe.

"You are the most intriguing lady of my acquaintance. I should very much like to know you more." He looked away as though to make it easier to refuse.

She bit her lip and blinked back the burning in her eyes. "I should like that as well."

His mouth dropped open just a bit. His eyes lit with warmth she had only seen directed to others. "I cannot offer you a dance, but would you care for a hand of cards? We might take supper together after that."

"It would be my pleasure."

He offered his arm.

Playing cards sounded very appealing indeed. Dancing was best left to other ladies.

Not Romantic

Chapter 1

September 29, 1811

"MRS. BENNET IS RIGHT, a single young man of good fortune—or any fortune at all, must be in want of a wife. How else will his home be managed and his comfort established?" Lady Lucas flipped out the folded sheet.

Charlotte caught the free end and smoothed it over the feather bed. It was inconvenient that their maid of all work had fallen pregnant. Even more inconvenient, the magistrate who had a long-standing quibble with Papa forbade him to discharge the maid. Now she could no longer work, Papa still had to pay her through her confinement and until she was churched. Then they might afford another girl. Until that happy day, they all had to contribute their share to getting things done. At least the tasks were distracting and kept Mama's mind off—

"Now that Netherfield Park is finally let, we must see about making ourselves acquainted with the family. I have heard he has five thousand a year. Five thousand!" Mama knelt beside the bed and tucked the sheets under the feather bed.

A man of that consequence would attract a great deal of attention.

"I know your father will do his duty by us. I trust you—"

"Mama, please!"

"I know you have little desire to speak of it. Still you must not allow past disappointments to interfere with your future."

"You do not understand."

"I understand you have been sulky and sullen. None of that is getting you any closer to finding a husband and home of your own. Set aside your pining now, and act responsibly toward all of us."

Something in the set of Mama's jaw and the glint in her eye promised there would be no arguing this time. Mama expected her to secure Netherfield's new tenant, no matter who he might be. Perhaps if he lived anywhere but there, Charlotte might be able to consider it. But Netherfield?

Her stomach churned, and she dashed from the room. She took up her basket and hastened out the back door.

Had Mama forgotten it was Michaelmas *and* Netherfield Park had been let once more?

Probably. She was apt to forget matters like that, especially if they threatened to get in the way of what she wanted.

And what she wanted was to be rid of Charlotte before she was irretrievably on the shelf.

But for that to happen, she would have to get to know another man, at least well enough for him to make her an offer. That might just prove well enough for him to break her heart, just as *he* had done.

Seven years proved insufficient to dull the memory or numb the pain.

She increased her pace to nearly a run. If she did not have a few moments to herself to bring it all under good regulation once more …. No, she did not need to think about the possibility of falling to pieces in front of the entire family.

Charlotte picked her way along the footpath to the small stream running behind Lucas Lodge. Her favorite place when the family first took the house, now she only visited at Michaelmas.

The stream once ran deep and swift though the little grove of trees. Now though, it meandered, stagnant, collecting algae and debris in the backwaters that lapped over tree roots and rocks.

She searched for the fallen log and found the mark he had carved. An 'R' and a 'C', intertwined, a reminder of what he intimated would come.

The elm had stood by the stream, stately and tall. The beauty masked the truth. The inner core had been ravaged by insects. It collapsed in the first big storm after the initials had been carved.

Like Roger did.

She dragged her sleeve over her eyes, blotting away the bleariness. Today she could see far more clearly than she had at one and twenty.

She opened her basket. Autumn flowers would fill it before she returned. That way none would ask why she had brought it. For now, it contained letters.

Roger's letters.

They had never been engaged. She should never have accepted them. Yet, when Mama and Papa, delighted in the attention he paid her, had turned the other way, it seemed harmless enough.

It was not.

A beetle scuttled across the initials. She brushed it aside and tested the surface of the log. It would hold, for now. This would be the last year she could sit here, beside those initials.

Nonetheless, she would return lest she forget the results of foolish infatuation and romantic notions.

Sept 29, 1804

Seven years ago today, the first letter came from Netherfield, just after the September assembly. Roger had danced the first and last dance with her.

How well you looked on my arm.

His sure, steady hand faded a little through the years. The edges of the paper frayed at the corners, and tear-stains dotted the bottom margin.

We are a handsome couple, you and I.

He had been right, they were.

I shall call upon you soon. I look forward to writing my family to say I have called upon one of his Majesty's knights.

He did call, a fortnight later.

That was the way of things with Roger Courtney. He did as he said he would, eventually.

After that, he called—when it suited him. Often enough to convince Mama and Papa that he was courting her. They never knew that for every time he called, she spent two days waiting at home, wondering if she had misunderstood his intentions. Just when she was ready to give up, he appeared again to reassure her of his ... of his what?

She opened the next two letters. How pleased he was to call on the daughter of the mayor. How grateful he was for Sir William's offer to make introductions for him at St. James. How pleased his parents were with the idea of him courting a respectable young lady.

She pushed a stray hair from her face. How strange. Was it possible? She had never noticed it before. Nowhere had he ever written of his feelings toward her.

She unfolded the remaining letters and smoothed them over her lap. Running her fingers along each word, she read the letters, twice. Prickly chills started at her scalp and progressed down her back. She closed her eyes and allowed her head to fall back, calling forth every memory of every conversation they shared.

The truth had always been there. Her romantic notions had covered it with a veil of fantasy, blinding her to the truth.

Roger had been in love—with himself, not her.

No wonder he abandoned Netherfield so easily when his distant cousin, the baronet, invited him to stay at the family home in London.

He wrote once from town, addressed to her father, of course.

My time in Hertfordshire was a pleasure. I hope to see you and your charming family again when next you come to court at St. James. Alas, I do not expect to return to Hertfordshire anytime soon, and must relinquish my lease on Netherfield. I shall always look fondly upon our acquaintance.

He never wrote again.

Underneath the letters lay a yellowed scrap of newspaper: the report of his marriage to a baronet's daughter, at Michaelmas, 1805.

She had wept that day and every Michaelmas since. But only on Michaelmas. It was her one concession to the romantic sensibilities she once entertained.

The whole affair had vexed Papa and left Mama livid. Over time, their tempers mellowed and none spoke of the autumn of 1804, almost as though it had never happened.

She folded each letter. Perhaps she should discard them, offer them to the fire. No, not yet. Until Netherfield had a married, long-term tenant, she needed them. Wrapping the letters in a plain scrap of muslin, she tucked them in the bottom of the basket. Later they would return to their spot in her little lock box, a reminder of the dangers of young men with wealth and good looks, who excited passionate effusions.

Romance was a luxury she did not need and certainly did not want. No, all she wanted was a comfortable home and a respectable man to go with it. Preferably not related to Netherfield Park. That place would never be comfortable to her.

She would go home by way of the lane where some lovely Michaelmas daisies and yellow crocus grew. Mama liked their brilliant colors for the parlor vases. None would think anything more of her Michaelmas sojourn.

October 15, 1811

Papa paid the expected calls on Netherfield's new tenant, a Mr. Bingley, and pronounced him an agreeable young man of good character. He stared directly at Charlotte as he said it. Much to Mama's distress, Mr. Bingley was off again to London before the rest of the family could make his acquaintance. He assured Papa he would return, with his party, in time for October's public assembly.

Charlotte kept her own counsel. Had she been asked, she would have been just as happy for the mysterious Mr. Bingley to stay away entirely. His presence, no matter his income, was not worth the fuss it added to her pre-assembly toilette.

"I cannot fathom the need to flit from one place to another, like a finch going hither and yon, never coming to roost." Mama peered into the looking glass and tucked another pin into Charlotte's hair. "He owes the neighborhood more than that. He is set up to be a leader of the fashionable set."

"Fashionable in Meryton?" Maria sniffed.

"He should be a leading example amongst us. With five thousand a year, he ought to know such things.

The neighborhood suffers when these gentlemen just up and leave without concern for those left behind."

"We have not even been introduced, Mama. He is nothing to us and his presence or absence does not signify." Charlotte fastened her grandmother's comb in her hair and turned away from the mirror.

Maria leaned forward on her hands. "I heard he was to return with a large party of friends. Twelve gentlemen and seven ladies—or perhaps it was the other way."

"No, no, it was five sisters and a cousin," Mama said.

"It might be eight goats and three mules for all we know—or perhaps no party at all. None of that changes the fact that it does not signify to us."

"How can you say it does not matter?" Maria's voice turned high and whiny. "For gentlemen are always in great demand at Assemblies. How delightful would it be for him to bring enough gentlemen that none should have to sit out."

"I do so hate to see you sit out. It is one of the worst things in the world." Mama adjusted the comb just a mite.

Everything had to be on Mama's terms. Charlotte clenched her hands not to move it back. Perhaps one day she would be good enough for Mama.

"And who knows what dancing with a wealthy man might lead to?"

Charlotte cringed and bit her tongue. Mama truly did not desire an answer, particularly an honest one.

"Let us depart." Papa called from somewhere downstairs.

The Master of Ceremonies should always be among the first to arrive.

Papa need not have worried. They arrived at the assembly rooms before most of the musicians.

The hall, with its Saxon blue walls and white trim, took on an entirely different character when empty: cold, aloof, and echoingly silent. Nothing like the warm, merry place it became when filled with dancers.

At Mama's insistence, Charlotte accompanied Papa at the door. What better way not to miss the arrival of the mysterious Mr. Bingley? In the meantime, Papa welcomed each arrival as if they were guests in his own home. Sometimes his overflowing goodwill seemed a bit excessive, but as vices went, it was a small enough one to excuse.

"Mr. Bingley!" Papa extended his hand as if to an old friend. "How good to see you. We wondered if you would return from your travels in time for our modest little gathering."

Mr. Bingley shook Papa's hand with equal enthusiasm. Perhaps they were kindred spirits.

Like Papa and Roger.

Her shoulders twitched. She adjusted her wrap, but the sensation remained.

"I love a country dance and anticipate enjoying several this evening. I would not countenance missing the first assembly since taking Netherfield. Indeed not. In fact, I have brought back a party of friends to add to the merriment. May I present Mr. Darcy, my friend from Derbyshire, my brother and sister, Mr. and Mrs. Hurst, and my other sister, Miss Bingley?"

Bows, curtsies and disdaining looks were exchanged. The ladies especially did not seem well-pleased. Their dresses bespoke their familiarity—and preference— for far finer company than they would encounter here.

"This is my eldest daughter." Papa propelled her forward with a firm hand on her shoulder. "Miss Charlotte Lucas."

She fought to catch her balance as she curtsied— no small feat considering.

Mr. Bingley bowed. "Very pleased to make your acquaintance, Miss Lucas. Are you engaged for the first dance?"

He was very handsome, especially when he smiled. She forced her features into a pleasant expression. "I am not so engaged."

"Would you the dance the first set with me?"

Not that she had any choice now. "I will, sir."

"Capital. Perhaps, if your good father can spare your company, you might introduce us about the room."

"What an excellent notion. I can certainly relinquish her for so noble a duty." Papa bowed and ushered them into the ballroom. Mr. Bingley and his sisters followed her though Mr. Hurst headed toward the refreshment tables, and Mr. Darcy was nowhere to be seen.

Even had he not had such a personable disposition, Mr. Bingley would have been easy to introduce. The denizens of Meryton all but lined up to meet him. He was uniformly good-natured and well-mannered to everyone, skilled at making everyone feel well liked.

Young ladies hovered about him, probably all hoping to be asked for the first dance.

How strange they should be envious of her in just a few moments.

Papa announced the first dance and Mr. Bingley led her to the dance floor. The opening notes, though, sounded a mite flat.

Mr. Bingley was the kind of partner not at all reluctant to meet her gaze and hold it steadily. His merry blue eyes, expressive face and nimble dance steps made it easy, far too easy, for a young lady to believe herself the object of intense interest. A dangerous dance floor illusion.

It was possible he was as he appeared. Not likely, but possible. Perhaps she should at least give him a chance.

The second dance of the set proceeded as agreeably as the first. The other girls had reason for envy. He was easily the best dancer there.

Mr. Bingley escorted her off the dance floor and excused himself to engage another partner for the next dance. Charlotte faded into the crowd and sagged against the wall. It was, after all, what he was expected to do. By the end of the night, half of Meryton would fancy themselves in love with him.

Eliza Bennet waved at her from the far side of the room and approached her straight away. "We have a fine company tonight, do we not?"

"Papa anticipated excellent attendance tonight."

"I fear Mama has already declared there to be too few gentlemen. I am glad you have come to keep me company, though. What do you think of the new tenant at Netherfield?"

"He is a good dancer."

"I noticed. But what do you think of him? You can hardly have danced the first set with him and not offer some further observation than the nimbleness of his footwork."

"He is a pleasant young man."

"Great praise from you!"

It was, in fact.

Eliza laughed. "Mr. Bingley seems well pleased with the assembly—even if the rest of his party is not. See how his sisters look down upon the rest of us. They strut like peacocks caught in a hen house."

"Is not this sort of event beneath their usual expectations?"

"Perhaps it is. Still, I think them very rude for not being more agreeable. Excuse me. I must join my next partner." Eliza hurried toward Lydia and Kitty, amidst a knot of young men.

Perhaps she was more in a hurry to check her sisters' romping behavior than find her partner. Probably best she should.

Charlotte wandered along the long wall. Miss Bingley and Mrs. Hurst were chatting to one another, neglected it would seem, by Meryton's male population. Had they no offers to dance, or had they refused them?

Yes, it was wrong to hope to overhear their conversation. But it could be most interesting.

She found a place to sit and admire the dancers, not far from Mr. Bingley's sisters.

"Oh, dear." Mrs. Hurst pointed her chin toward the dance floor. "Charles has that look in his eyes again."

"Who is he dancing with? Do you know?"

"I believe it is one of the Miss Bennets, Miss Jane Bennet."

"What sort of a girl is she?" Miss Bingley squared her shoulders. "As I understand, her father is in possession of a modest estate just a few miles from town. So she is a gentlewoman, of sorts."

Mrs. Hurst's lips worked into a very distinct and pronounced frown. "It looks as though Charles may have found another one of his 'angels'."

"Did you expect any less? That is his way. I grant you, this might be a little quick even for him, but he always finds the prettiest girl to fawn over. Miss Bennet certainly fits his preferences."

"So now I suppose we will be expected to entertain her until he tires of her, or finds a prettier girl to smile at."

"I have heard she is thought a very agreeable, good kind of girl. Let us just hope she proves as agreeable in the drawing room as she is on the dance floor."

"Or that he moves on to another angel as quickly as he did the last time." Mrs. Hurst chuckled and led them off toward the refreshments.

Poor Jane, she had no idea of the heartache lying in store for her. But then again, she might not be so easily touched and remain safe. A word of warning might be in order, though. Mr. Bingley was cut from the same cloth as Roger.

At least all temptation to like him was now past, and she could meet him anywhere as an indifferent acquaintance. His charm and smile held no further appeal.

❧

October 23, 1811

A se'nnight later, Eliza appeared a quarter of an hour early for Lady Lucas's carefully planned dinner party. Charlotte hurried her to the morning room to be out of the way of the final preparations.

Eliza dropped inelegantly into the nearest chair. She threw her head back and huffed out a great breath, an expression Mrs. Bennet despised. "We have been several times now to Netherfield, and I do not know what to make of it. Jane and I seem welcome enough, but the 'superior sisters' make their opinion of the rest of our family quite obvious. Even worse, I seem to be the only one to notice it."

"Why do you continue to call upon them if you find it so disagreeable?"

"I am quite certain Mr. Bingley admires Jane. For her part, Jane gives every evidence of yielding to the preference and is in a way to be very much in love."

Jane in love with Mr. Bingley? Had she any idea of what heartbreak she courted?

"Do you believe his sisters object?"

"I doubt they are much aware. Jane is so discreet in all her interactions. She unites a great strength of feeling, composure of temper and a uniform cheerfulness of manner. All of which guards her from the suspicions of the impertinent."

"Are you certain of Jane's feelings for him?"

"You know she is not one to speak of such things, but I am convinced."

But was Mr. Bingley? A man so easily distracted could not be trusted to his own devices. Roger certainly could not.

Charlotte leaned against the table's edge near Eliza. "Have you considered sometimes it is a disadvantage to be so very guarded? If a woman conceals her affection with the same skill from the object of it, she may lose the opportunity of fixing him. It will then be but poor consolation to believe the world equally in the dark. Very few of us have heart enough to be really in love without encouragement. In nine cases out of ten, a woman had better show more affection than she feels. Mr. Bingley likes your sister undoubtedly. He may never do more than like her, if she does not help him on."

"She does help him on, as much as her nature will allow. If *I* can perceive her regard for him, he must be a simpleton indeed not to discover it too."

"Remember, Eliza, that he does not know Jane's disposition as you do."

"If a woman is partial to a man, and does not endeavor to conceal it, he must find it out."

"Perhaps he must, if he sees enough of her—and has no one working to influence his opinions. Though Mr. Bingley and Jane meet tolerably often, it is never for many hours together. Jane should therefore make the most of every half hour in which she can command his attention. When she is secure of him, there will be leisure for falling in love as much as she chooses."

Eliza looked up at her, brows knit tight. "Your plan is a good one where nothing is in question but the desire of being well married. If I were determined to get a rich husband, or any husband, I dare say I should adopt it. But these are not Jane's feelings. She has known him only a fortnight. She danced four dances with him at Meryton. She saw him one morning at his own house, and has since dined in company with him four times. This is not quite enough to make her understand his character."

"Had she merely dined with him, she might only have discovered whether he had a good appetite. You must remember that four evenings have been also spent together. Four evenings may do a great deal."

"Yes, these four evenings have enabled them to ascertain that they both like Vingt-un better than Commerce. With respect to any other leading characteristic, I do not imagine that much has been unfolded."

"I wish Jane success with all my heart." Charlotte pushed off the table and wandered across the room.

How little Eliza understood the ways of young men.

"If she were married to him tomorrow, I should think she had as good a chance of happiness as if she studied his character for a twelvemonth."

Eliza's jaw dropped. Did her eyes hurt when they bulged that way?

"Happiness in marriage is entirely a matter of chance. If the dispositions of the parties are ever so well known to each other, or ever so similar beforehand, it does not advance their felicity in the least. They always contrive to grow sufficiently unlike afterwards to have their share of vexation. It is better to know as little as possible of the defects of the person with whom you are to pass your life."

"You make me laugh, Charlotte, but it is not sound. You know it is not sound, and that you would never act in this way yourself, would you?"

Charlotte shrugged. What point in arguing? When Eliza held so strong an opinion, little would change her mind. She had not Charlotte's experience to sway her way of thinking.

Perhaps she should tell Eliza about Roger, that might…no, not even to Eliza. Some things did indeed need to remain firmly in the past. If Eliza thought

Jane had a chance with Mr. Bingley, who was she to interfere?

Eliza's question was a good one though. If the opportunity came, would she have the courage to follow good sense and do as she recommended Jane do—marry for purely practical consideration, without regard to sentiment or regard? It was one thing to offer the advice, but entirely another to act upon it herself.

But if it was good sense for Jane, whose prospects were much better, then it was even better advice for herself.

Would she act this way herself?

Yes. She would.

✣Chapter 2

CHARLOTTE STARED AT THE torn shirt in her hand. This was the third time John's shirt had found its way to her mending basket. All for the same reason. Would he and James never stop with practicing fisticuffs with their mates? The bruised faces and torn shirts hardly made their appearances more manly and certainly did not impress any of the young ladies in the neighborhood.

How kind of him to engage in a useless lark that made more work for her. Unfeeling, ungrateful creature. She might just leave his shirt as it was, but he might well not notice and wear it out to Mama's suffering and humiliation.

She huffed and stabbed her needle into the fabric. Best get on with it while the light in the morning room was still good.

"Charlotte! Charlotte!" Maria dashed in and closed the door behind her. She flung herself into the chair next to Charlotte and leaned in close. "Such news as I have heard from town. You will never guess."

"As I am sure you are going to tell me, might you at least move out of the light so I may finish this?"

"You will not be such a crosspatch when you hear my news." Maria untied her bonnet and tossed it on the table. "Mama and I went into town this morning."

"I am quite aware as you failed to invite me, despite knowing I had errands to run myself."

"Oh what a termagant you are. For that, I should not tell you anything, but it is all so delicious. I cannot keep it to myself."

"Ouch!" Charlotte pulled the needle from her finger and sucked off a drop of blood. "Then tell me lest the distraction cause me even more serious injury."

"We saw officers in town, with lovely red coats and boots. Oh! I have never seen such men before."

"Do not be a goosecap. You have seen soldiers before."

"Well, perhaps I have, but I never noticed them before. They were nearly as fine as the party from Netherfield."

"I rejoice with you that your scenery was pleasant."

"That is not the best part! The girl at the grocer said the baker said the innkeeper said that the regiment was coming to Meryton! We shall have a whole camp full of soldiers among us very soon!" Maria bounced with each word.

Lovely.

It was not enough that Netherfield's lease brought new gentlemen among them. Now they would be plagued with officers exciting Maria's flirtations.

"Do not get your hopes up too very high. We know nothing about these officers and what kind of men they might be. Not all of them are as fine as their coats."

"Must you spoil my fun? I do not mean to marry a soldier. But the flirtation is great fun! I know Kitty and Lydia will be just wild when I tell them. What a delicious piece of excitement for the winter."

"Need I caution you against excessive flirtation? It would not do to harm your reputation."

"You sound like Mama and I would that you would stop it. If you do not like that news, perhaps you will prefer this." Maria leaned her face very close to Charlotte's. "The Bennets received a houseguest today. Millie met their girl, Betsy, in town. She said it is Mr. Bennet's cousin—the one to whom Longbourn is entailed."

"Heavens! I expect they must be very uncomfortable indeed. I thought them not to be on speaking terms these many years."

"Millie says Betsy said that was the elder Mr. Collins and he is now dead. The younger Mr. Collins has been made a vicar now and wants to make peace in the family."

"He must be a very amiable young man then to make such a journey—"

"All the way from Kent."

"—from Kent, to promote reconciliation. I am disposed to think well of him already."

"Well, I dare say you will not when you hear this. He arrived with marriage in mind. His patroness deemed he should marry. So, he is looking for a wife amongst his cousins to 'right the wrong done them by the entail.'"

"Why would I dislike him for so noble a gesture? What greater kindness could he offer them? I think even more highly of him now."

Maria crossed her arms and huffed. "How unromantic to be married for such a reason."

"Perhaps, but very practical and sensible. It behooves you to begin thinking more realistically."

"I do not need another of your lectures. Gentlemen would like you so much more if you were not so drab and dull, and always thinking." Maria snatched her bonnet and stormed out.

Charlotte tossed her mending on the table and cradled her face in her hands.

No one said life was fair, but this was too much to be borne. How was it her friends had all the good fortune—born with beauty and status and wealth. Now a cousin riding in, willing to marry one of them for purely noble reasons, not having even met them first.

When would someone appear desiring to marry her because he wanted a steady, practical, dependable wife—not caring if she was pretty or rich or young? She bit her knuckle, her insides roiling like an iron cauldron.

No, no, it would not do to dwell upon any of this. It would only add to her own misery. Who would want to keep company with her then? The vicar had said on Sunday that the sun shone both upon the just and the unjust. Railing against it would change nothing. Best choose to be content in whatever her circumstance.

It was the right thing to do.

It was the only thing she could do.

———❧———

November 19, 1811

Kitty and Lydia arrived early the next day, full of news and high spirits. Maria welcomed them into the parlor where Charlotte and Mama were already established, sewing and writing letters.

"So is it true, the militia are come?" Maria braced her elbows on her knees and leaned in close to Lydia.

"Indeed they are." Kitty tittered behind her hand.

"And with them so many agreeable officers." Lydia jumped to her feet.

"You have met them already?" Maria asked.

"Indeed we have," Kitty said.

"Mama went to greet Mrs. Forster, the Colonel's wife, and we went along with her. The colonel and his officers were there, and we met them all."

"But how? Surely your father had not time to call upon the colonel." Maria's eyes bulged.

"They already met you see, at the wine sellers, I think, or perhaps the tobacconist. It does not matter, for they were already acquainted when Mrs. Forster arrived."

Maria huffed.

"Oh do not be cross with us. It is not our fault, Mama happened to call upon them first. Our Aunt Philips will host a party to which they will all be invited. You will certainly meet them then." Kitty patted Maria's arm.

"And it will be all the better then for I expect we may impose upon Mary to play for us. Then, we may dance with them all." Lydia threw her arms in the air.

"And there will not be so many young ladies present, so we might have them to ourselves!"

Maria clapped. "What a wonderful thought. Were any of them handsome?"

"Or steady or reliable?" Charlotte called, not looking up from her sewing.

"They were handsome and agreeable." Kitty rolled her eyes in the familiar Bennet sort of way.

"Especially Denny and Sanderson, and the most pleasing of them all, Mr. Wickham." Lydia's cheeks colored.

"He is tall and dark and well-mannered and very congenial."

Lydia clasped her hands before her. "And I will introduce you—but you must remember I saw him first."

"He is so very agreeable, he makes up for our cousin, Mr. Collins." Kitty flopped back against her chair.

"He is simply dreadful." Lydia hid her face in her hands. "Supercilious, sanctimonious, and so superior."

Somehow it was not very surprising that Lydia should not find such a man pleasing. Her criticism was probably more compliment than anything else.

"Because of his patroness, the great Lady Catherine de Bourgh." Kitty thrust her nose in the air and sniffed. "With her estate in Kent. That is nearly all he talks about. And he never stops talking. He will be at

Aunt Philips's party tomorrow night. You can hear him waffle on about how Lady Catherine wants him to get a wife and how he means to do just that."

"He is so very pious for the sake of mending the rift among our families. He has decided to choose a wife from among his cousins!" Lydia rolled her eyes.

"One of us! Can you imagine Lydia or I a vicar's wife?"

"It is a very respectable profession and an honorable role in life." Even for an imperfect man.

"You sound like Mary and Mama." Lydia sneered.

"I dare say Sister Mary would make the best match for him. She is every bit as dull as he."

"And she loves Fordyce almost as much as he." Lydia giggled into her hand. "But there is very little chance of Mary getting him. He thinks himself too good for the likes of a very plain middle daughter. He wants Jane—"

"But she is got by Mr. Bingley—"

"So he will have to settle for—"

"Lizzy!" They collapsed on each other in peals of laughter.

Lydia sat up very straight and puffed her chest. "I am very sensible, madam, of the hardship to my fair cousins and could say much on the subject. I am cautious of appearing forward and precipitate, though. I can assure the young ladies that I come prepared to admire them. At present I will not say more, but perhaps when we are better acquainted –"

"What other conclusion could you draw from that?"

"Is it not the greatest joke?" Lydia laughed.

How could they ridicule so ideal a circumstance— everything Charlotte could hope for or dream of?

She rose, fist clenched against her tremor. "I do not see how you consider any of this a joke. How do you think you will get along if you do not marry? How—tell me how? Surely you laugh now with your flirtations and fine red coats—but what will you do a few years hence when they are gone and your romantic notions have all led to naught? Perhaps then a man like Mr. Collins might look very appealing indeed." She threw down her sewing and stormed from the room.

Air, she needed fresh air. She dashed out and did not stop until the house was hid from view.

How could this be? Had Eliza any idea of the extent of her good fortune? This cousin, the antithesis of men like Roger and Mr. Bingley, casually cast aside for not being agreeable enough?

But then again, Eliza was well aware of the desperation of her family's situation. She was apt to speak a great deal, but at the heart, she was sensible. Perhaps he had already demonstrated some great flaw of character making his suit entirely untenable. Perhaps he was cruel, or dishonest, or immoral.

Eliza was no fool; there had to be some excellent reason for her to find him so repulsive. Kitty and Lydia must simply be too silly to see it themselves. A man who offered so much surely had to be beyond the pale to be so easily rejected.

Tomorrow she would know firsthand. Then she might put an end to the gnawing jealousy that raised its head every time Eliza or Mr. Collins were mentioned.

November 20, 1811

"Thank you so much for inviting us." Lady Lucas kissed Mrs. Philips's cheeks.

Charlotte turned away. It was always uncomfortable watching Mama express more warmth than she felt.

"It is always a pleasure to host your distinguished husband and your lovely daughters." Mrs. Philips stepped back and gestured to a tall, heavy-looking young man.

He could not be less than five and twenty, but his grave, stately manner lent him a mature air. He bowed, a stiff, precise movement that had surely been rehearsed to perfection.

"Permit me to introduce a new member of our acquaintance, Mr. Bennet's cousin, Mr. Collins. He is vicar to Lady Catherine de Bourgh of Rosings Park."

"We are pleased to make your acquaintance, sir." Lady Lucas tapped Charlotte with her elbow and they curtsied. "Has Mrs. Collins come with you?"

Charlotte winced. Yes, it was an innocent, appropriate question, but when one knew the answer already, was it necessary?

"There is currently no Mrs. Collins, madam, though my esteemed patroness has instructed me that I should find a bride soon."

"Well, you have come to an excellent place to find one, sir. There are many lovely eligible girls here in Meryton, including my dear Charlotte."

Mrs. Philips pressed her lips, and gave Mama a decidedly sour look.

Why did she say such a thing? Charlotte's face burned hotter than the many candles in the drawing room. With essentially no dowry, she was hardly eligible. None but the dearest, most generous of her friends would call her lovely. No, she was at best plain and practical.

All Mama had managed to convey was a sense of desperation.

What joy.

Mr. Collins smiled at her, that same conciliatory smile offered her by the matrons of Meryton. "It is a pleasure to meet you in person. My fair cousins have told me about their most amiable friend."

"My nieces are indeed very dear, kind girls, are they not?" Mrs. Philips turned up her nose just a mite. With no daughters of her own, she was every bit as attentive in promoting the Bennet girls' fortunes as their own mother.

Charlotte could hardly begrudge her friends their supporters. It was not their fault that there were not enough men for all the single young ladies. No, they all might thank Napoleon for that favor.

More guests pushed through the front door. Mrs. Philips excused herself and dragged Mr. Collins away for more introductions.

Mama pulled out her fan and drew Charlotte into the drawing room. "Since you have forsworn Mr. Bingley, you should consider him. Mr. Collins would be a very suitable match for you."

"You well know his intentions. It could hardly be seemly to throw myself at him under the circumstances." Not to mention whatever Eliza had discovered to make her dislike him so.

"I am not so certain the opinions he states are his own. I suspect they are ones given to him by his patroness; his desires for ease and comfort; and the artful suggestions of Mrs. Bennet."

Charlotte's eyes bulged. Pray, no one was looking her way now! "How can you say such things? You only just met the man."

"I may have only just met *this* man. But, I have known a great many men. Have you forgotten my nine brothers? Trust me. I recognize a simple, easily-governed man when I see one. Mr. Collins is exactly one of that sort. You would do very well with him, indeed."

"But he is not—"

Mama grasped Charlotte's wrist hard. "What he says is entirely separate from what he will do. Jane is all but spoken for. He will not have the spleen to challenge for her and can you see him with Eliza? She would not have him even if he had the bollocks to ask."

"Mama!"

"Forgive me, dear. You are quite right." She sucked in a deep breath and straightened her shoulders. "Still though, I do not think even Mrs. Bennet and the threat of destitution could bring Mr. Collins and Eliza together. Which brings us to Mary." Mama glanced about the room.

She need not have bothered. A quick listen located Mary at the pianoforte.

"Mary is your true rival for him. It is to your disadvantage that she plays and sings and studies Fordyce, gah! She is a dreadful bore, whilst you have a charming disposition and practicality a man in his circumstances would value."

"You think him a man of good character?"

"As good as any. Do you think he could have earned the approbation of a patroness if he harbored some ugly secret? You may trust me on this. It is Eliza's stubbornness, not his shortcomings, that will keep them apart. Our one hope is that Mrs. Bennet ignores Mary as she usually does, so Mr. Collins does not turn to her when Eliza refuses him."

"I cannot believe you would be planning his choice of bride within minutes of meeting him, much less instructing me on how to steal a prospect from my best friend."

Mama clenched her hand and fluttered her fan a little faster. "Go and watch your friend, and you will see clear as I do. You will do her a favor, diverting his attentions from her. It is obvious she does not want them. Go, go." She shooed Charlotte away. "Mrs. Goulding, how lovely to see you this evening…"

Charlotte slipped away and skirted along the edge of the room. Would there ever be a day for her to stand with the others, making them feel welcome in her own home?

People clustered in groups around the drawing room, making small talk and sharing pleasantries. Eliza was engaged with several of the officers and Lydia and Kitty. Probably just as well, all things considered. It was not as if she could walk up to Eliza and ask her opinions. In that, Mama offered sound advice. Best she attempt to draw her own conclusions.

Mr. Collins approached the group, apparently eager to engage them in conversation. Eliza's countenance lost its bloom. She really must learn not to roll her eyes so. Perhaps she considered herself discreet, but at least to a dedicated observer, she was not.

Mr. Collins, though, appeared oblivious to the amused reactions he garnered, not just from Eliza, but from all within earshot. Did he possess good manners or a level of unawareness rarely seen outside the very young? Both were certainly a possibility.

Miss Long took Mary's place at the pianoforte, and the entire company paused briefly to take note.

Eliza approached her, hands extended. "Oh, Charlotte, how I missed your company."

"Indeed? You seemed to enjoy at least some of your conversation a great deal."

Eliza glanced over her shoulder toward the corner where Mr. Wickham chatted with Lydia and Kitty. "Some of it has been quite pleasing. Have you been introduced to my cousin, Mr. Collins, yet?"

"We were introduced when we arrived." Charlotte tipped her head toward the fireplace.

Mr. Collins, Mrs. Bennet and Mrs. Philips gathered there, speaking far too loudly.

So, that particular mannerism was not confined to the Gardiner branch of the family. For all his propensity to judge failures of propriety, Mr. Bennet's family was not without its transgressors.

"So then you have heard a great deal about the wonders of Lady Catherine de Bourgh and Rosings Park in Kent." Eliza rolled her eyes.

"I believe he made mention of his pleasing circumstances."

"You are too kind, Charlotte, far too kind."

"I cannot think it a good thing to so quickly form a prejudice against one I have only just met."

"After a full two days in his company—and I do mean two *full* days—I believe I have sufficient grounds to declare him a unique and peculiar man."

"But would not his patroness's approbation suggest—"

"Yes, I suppose you make an excellent case. I will allow him to be a tolerably good fellow, quite unlikely to cause harm to anyone." Eliza's cheek dimpled and she cast about the room. "It seems Maria has wasted no time becoming acquainted with the officers."

"Few young ladies seem immune to their charms."

"Unfortunately my mother is among those still." Eliza fluttered her hand before her face in an amazing imitation of Mrs. Bennet. "I had quite a fondness for a red coat in my day."

Charlotte giggled.

"I know, I know, I should not speak so. Forgive me. I am not quite myself."

Mrs. Philips bustled up to them. "We are short a player for a hand of whist. Can I persuade you to join us, Lizzy?"

Eliza's eyes widened and she glanced about the room like an animal trapped.

"I should very much enjoy a hand of cards." Charlotte dipped her head at Eliza and made her way to the card table where Papa and Mr. Collins already chatted amiably.

Eliza mouthed a tiny 'thank you' and scurried off whilst Mrs. Philips sputtered.

"Are you going to join us at cards, Charlotte, dear?" Papa asked. "I did not think you would prefer cards to a conversation."

"Mrs. Philips suggested you might be in need of another player to fill out the table." She sat down. Best not to acknowledge the tension that radiated from her hostess in waves like heat from a hob.

"Indeed we are." Mrs. Philips sat across from Mr. Collins and handed him a deck of cards.

Their white backs bore stains and some of the edges were worn. Mr. Collins shuffled awkwardly, but at least he did not drop the cards.

"My patroness, Lady Catherine de Bourgh makes it a point to open a new deck of cards for every card table she hosts. She is the soul of generosity."

Mrs. Philips smiled a tightly strained expression that seemed to reflect patience more than good humor. Eliza wore the same expression at times.

"Rosings Park, we are given to understand is a very fine place, indeed," Mrs. Philips muttered.

"I am sure it is, very sure," Papa said.

"I do not mean to draw ill comparisons to your very fine establishment. By no means. I feel quite as if I have been welcomed to the small and intimate breakfast parlor at Rosings. Lady Catherine favors that room in the spring and summer."

Mrs. Philips feathers ruffled, and she twitched like an angry hen.

"Pray, madam, you must understand the chimney-piece alone in her favorite drawing room cost eight hundred pounds. Her taste is the most refined and elegant in all of England, to be sure. It is indeed the highest compliment I might offer to compare any-thing favorably with Rosings. I regard it the highest of condescension that she herself planned all the im-provements in my own humble abode."

The tension in Mrs. Philips's shoulders eased. "Oh, now I see. I had misunderstood your intent, but I do understand there was no slight intended at all."

So, Mr. Collins was not entirely insensitive to the feelings of others. Had Eliza recognized that?

Mrs. Philips tapped the table. "Perhaps we should play, Mr. Collins?"

"Perhaps so, but I should like to hear more about Rosings and your establishment there." Charlotte leaned forward a little.

Mrs. Philips's brows rose. "Miss Lucas, you are all politeness and curiosity."

"Charlotte certainly knows how to make people feel welcome. The spit and image of her mother, the consummate hostess."

"Papa, it is not seemly to offer such compliments, particularly in public." Charlotte's cheeks burned.

At least Papa was all kindness and affability. Unlike Mr. Bennet.

"Your humility does you credit, Miss Lucas. It is after all one of the chief of virtues in a young woman." Mr. Collins handed the shuffled deck to Mrs. Philips.

A warm little place filled within her heart. Compliments like his were so rare.

"Lady Catherine has been so generous and solicitous to my well-being. She is so attentive to such things you know. No detail in the parsonage is below her notice. She even saw to the fitting of the closet with shelves. Everything is arranged with all proper attention to my station, neither too high nor too low. Imagine my relief—for I am a bachelor and know little of keeping an establishment— to know everything is in right and proper order." Mr. Collins's chest puffed up a little, and he picked up his hand.

How interesting that he knew his own limitations and rightly valued the role of household management. Certainly Mr. Bennet did not.

As they played, he continued his glowing descriptions of the work done on his home and the generosity of his patroness.

To be sure, abundant elements of the ridiculous surrounded every word he said. But through that, an undertone of satisfaction, even joy in the situation of his life spoke as well.

How very agreeable to be so satisfied so early in one's life. He was fortunate to be so young and already so settled, and in such a pleasant-sounding situation.

"Mr. Collins, the suit is hearts." Mrs. Philips rapped the card on the table.

"Forgive me, madam." Tiny beads of sweat dotted his upper lip. "I know little of the game at present. I shall be glad to improve myself to learn more if you will but instruct me."

Charlotte folded her hand and placed it on the table. "Perhaps we should begin again and change partners. Papa is an excellent player, and I am not at all opposed to assisting a less certain player through the finer parts of the game."

Mrs. Philips bristled, eyes glittering like a hen about to peck. "There is no need—"

"What a very generous and thoughtful offer. I should hate to be a strain upon our generous hostess's good graces." He rose.

Papa did like-wise and changed places with him. Mrs. Philips muttered protests but Papa gathered the old hand up, shuffled and re-dealt the game.

Charlotte picked up her cards and smiled at Mr. Collins.

Some of the tension in his face eased, and he settled more comfortably in his seat.

She played her first card, along with a mild comment about the rules of play.

Mrs. Philips huffed under her breath, but Mr. Collins nodded, granted a bit too vigorously, and on his next turn, played very well indeed.

A little congratulation, a subtle reminder of rules now and then, and an occasional raised eyebrow or tap on the table rendered him a tolerable player.

Was he naturally observant and pliable, or hungry to be given an example of right conduct? Not that it particularly mattered, both were agreeable qualities.

At the end of the rubber, Mary Bennet moved to the piano in the corner. Lydia and Maria demanded she play a tune for dancing.

"I think dancing, in a private home, such as this, in so affable a company, to be a very appropriate occupation for young persons."

"I find dancing quite agreeable." Charlotte stood.

Mr. Collins scanned the room. Eliza was already lining up with one of the officers and Jane with Charlotte's own brother.

The corner of Mr. Collins' eyes drooped just a mite.

Rejection was hard, even when you never actually asked.

Jane looked toward them. "We need another couple for the set."

"Would you care to dance, Miss Lucas?" he asked, still staring at Eliza and Jane.

Yes, Eliza and Jane were the prettiest, most eligible girls in the neighborhood, and they were his cousins who would suffer when he inherited Longbourn. It was entirely right and proper he should look to them first.

But they did not seem to like him and she...well, she just might. She took his arm on the way to the impromptu dance floor. Eliza and Jane certainly had first claims on Mr. Collins's interests, but if they relinquished them…it might be a pleasing possibility. At least more so than being alone.

November 22, 1811

Several days later, Elizabeth arrived with a basket of pickles and preserves and carefully penned receipts.

Mama examined each jar. "I had no idea your mother would send samples to go along with the receipts I asked for. She is such a thoughtful neighbor."

"The reciept comes from her mother and grandmother. She is ever so protective of it. She wanted to make sure you knew how it was supposed to taste when you went to make your own." Elizabeth handed her the receipts.

Mama cleared her throat. Her face puckered as though she had drunk the pickling juice straight from the jar.

"For my tastes though, I have found the ginger too strong and the vinegar too sharp. I hope you will share with me your improvements on both if I promise not to tell my mother."

Mama's smile returned. "It will be our secret. Excuse me now whilst I take these to the kitchen." She trundled off, eyes on one of the receipts as she walked.

No doubt she was already formulating her plans to alter the taste.

"You are such a dreadful tease, Eliza."

"I fear my family gives me great fodder for it. I dare you to contradict me. My mother is excessively careful of the Gardiner family receipts. I think your mother is the only one outside the family with whom she has shared them."

"I think it quite dear that she should try so diligently to honor her mother's memory."

"Honoring a memory is a fine thing indeed, but I do not see how steadfastly adding more ginger than anyone— including herself—prefers honors anyone's memory. We all dread the appearance of those pickles on the table. I swear to you every one of us tastes ginger every time Grandmother Gardiner is mentioned."

Charlotte snickered.

"You laugh, but you agree."

"Even if I do, you must concede not everyone has the same tastes. I am sure someone likes those pickles. I believe my father does."

"That is very well and good both for your father and my grandmother's memory. But I am quite glad to have them remain on the still room shelves."

"You might not think so if, in the dead of winter you found them the only thing on your shelves. Then you might appreciate them and find them very good tasting indeed."

"I do not know who you sound more like, Jane or Mary. Either way, you are a good and dear creature. I am made better for our acquaintance."

"Now you are teasing me." Charlotte wagged her finger.

"Not at all, you are a sweet friend to me. I have not yet thanked you for rescuing me at my Aunt Philips's party."

"Rescuing you?"

"You kept Mr. Collins occupied and in excellent humor the whole of the evening. And most importantly, away from me and the rest of my sisters."

"I imagine it rather dreary to have his company in your home and then again when you are out. Rather like sitting with one's husband at a dinner party I expect."

Eliza threw her head back. "Oh, Charlotte, you have no idea."

"He is not a good guest? Does not your mother's hospitality transform anyone into a most appreciative guest."

"Oh, he is appreciative, to be sure."

"You are displeased?" Charlotte bit her lip, as much in anticipation of Eliza's answer as to quell her own urge to say more.

"It is not just me. He is driving us all to distraction. Even Jane has taken up strange habits to avoid him. Imagine her inviting Lydia to help her call upon the tenants in an effort to avoid his otherwise constant society. I will tell you, though, she has since given up that particular strategy. The last time Mr. Collins declared it entirely appropriate for himself as a clergyman to condole with those less fortunate and accompanied them on all their calls. Jane spent the rest of the day abed of a sick headache! Even Papa, who delights in the ridiculous, has grown tired of him. He has suddenly developed a penchant for shooting which you know he has never had before. He leaves early and inevitably returns empty-handed. I saw him secret a book into the hamper he packed with him."

"You are too cruel. You make him out to be some kind of blackguard."

"To be fair, he is by no means a villain. But, Mr. Collins is the most ridiculous man I have ever met. I hope never to encounter another like him, or I shall go quite distracted."

"I am sure if you were but a little more patient with him, you would find him less disagreeable."

"But that would require time spent in his presence, the thing I most seek to avoid." Eliza clutched her temples and covered her face with her hand.

"What is wrong?"

"Please do not dismiss me or tell me how foolish I am. I believe myself in great danger from Mr. Collins."

"Danger? Do you suspect him of violence?"

"No, no, not that. I believe, that is I have become suspicious, that he and Mama have been making plans. His express purpose is to find a wife to bring back to his patroness in Kent."

"I had heard something to that effect."

"Mama thinks it a very good idea and is happy to promote our virtues at every opportunity. Dear Jane is exempt of course, as Mama has hopes of her and Mr. Bingley. On the other hand, I have never been complimented so much as when Mr. Collins is in hearing. It is a very strange transformation in Mama who has never been effusive in her praise to me."

"You doubt her sincerity?"

"More, I doubt her motives. Mr. Collins has begun looking at me. I see him staring at me from the far side of the room quite often now. Mama has increased her praise to truly embarrassing levels. Just this morning, she made note of how prettily I blinked."

Charlotte sniggered.

"I wish I were exaggerating, but Jane will tell you the same. I was mortified."

"That does seem a bit excessive."

"I try to keep it all at arm's end with humor and good will. I fear he may be forming plans which might be far less agreeable to me than to Mama."

"You believe he wants to—"

"Do not say it, pray, do not say. I dread that giving voice to the notion could bring it to pass all the sooner."

"I hardly know what to say. Many women would be pleased for such attention."

Very, very pleased.

"I suspect my sister Mary would. I often see her trying to attract his attentions. But Mama will not allow for it. She is determined he should have me." She laughed, but it faded off into a melancholy note. "Both Jane and I have always dreamt that we might marry for love. It is difficult to contemplate a husband whose presence I can hardly tolerate."

"I understand your hopes, but unless there is a great defect of character involved, a steady income and a respectable profession are very agreeable qualities, as are honesty and transparency. He has been very open about his intentions."

"But I do not even like him. Not at all. I cannot even imagine myself liking him. What am I to do?"

What indeed? Somehow telling her to stop being foolish and consider her good fortune did not seem to be the advice Eliza would want. And with Jane's apparent success with Mr. Bingley, bringing up her heartbreak with Roger would surely fall on deaf ears.

As much as she disliked Eliza's distress, it was, in a way, good news. If Eliza truly did not want him, then he might just be open to someone whose hopes and desires were more in line with his own.

❧ Chapter 3

November 26, 1811

THE NIGHT OF THE Netherfield Ball, Mama pulled Charlotte aside just after she finished dressing. "Your gown looks very well indeed."

"I am glad you are pleased, Mama."

"It is a shame we must give up hopes of Mr. Bingley—"

Charlotte cringed. Pray not another lecture about her failure to attract Mr. Bingley's eye. At least she had 'lost' him to worthy competition. Few could stand in Jane's shadow and not be outshone.

"—but his preference is very clear. Mr. Collins however—"

"Is quite set upon Eliza."

"Whilst that may be true for now, he certainly seems to enjoy keeping company with you. Remember the Philips's party? You did very well together.

What is more—and perhaps most significant—Eliza has no preference for him herself. That should free your conscience and permit you to take full advantage of any available opportunity."

"You make this sound like a military campaign."

"My dear, a ballroom is a battlefield of sorts, and I do not wish you going out unprepared. Consider what it is you wish for and take every occasion to pursue it."

Much as she hated the sound of it, Mama was right. Mr. Collins was the first man of her acquaintance whose views toward marriage were so practical. How much better matched in expectation and temperament could they be? Moreover, he showed himself considerate toward the needs and desires of others. What more could she desire in a man?

Eliza made it clear she experienced no warm sentiments toward him. It was difficult to believe, though. How could she not? The great boon he offered her family, the honor he offered her. Somehow, all her romantic notions blinded her to the world's harsh realities. But then again perhaps reality was not so hard when one was not considered on the shelf.

If Eliza could not appreciate Mr. Collins's finer qualities, perhaps Charlotte should make herself available as someone who did.

<hr />

Since Papa was not required as Master of Ceremonies, Mama insisted they not arrive so early as to be the first ones there. A small crowd had already gathered in the retiring rooms when they arrived.

Charlotte barely found a place to sit and don her dancing slippers. She edged and shouldered her way through the press, past the greeting line of Bingleys, and into the ballroom. Finally, she could draw a breath, albeit a small one.

The entire upper society of Meryton must be making their appearance here. The best dressed among them were the Netherfield party, but as they were fresh from London, one hardly expected anything else. Still, not a few were clothed well enough to meet even the superior sisters' satisfaction.

"So you finished the new trims on your gown after all." Eliza sidled past two officers and slipped into a tiny open space beside Charlotte.

"Are they to your liking?" Charlotte held her skirt out.

"Very much so. I could not envision it when you described it to me, but it looks very well indeed."

"Your approbation is always very welcome."

Eliza chuckled. "Listen to you, so very formal, almost as though we had not been friends all our lives."

"Quite befitting the event, is it not?"

"Certainly some of the company here seems to think so."

"You mean Mr. Darcy?" Charlotte looked over her shoulder.

Mr. Darcy stood in his usual place at the edge of the room. So tall, he was easy to find among the rest of the guests.

"I do indeed. I am not certain I can forgive him for destroying the happiness of so many here tonight by keeping Mr. Wickham away."

"You cannot mean that. I know you are disposed to dislike him, but you cannot assign him so much blame."

"I can and I do, but let us not continue to speak of something entirely disagreeable, when something only somewhat disagreeable might do. Mr. Collins continues to enjoy his stay with us at Longbourn."

"I am pleased you are at last enjoying his visit."

"I said he is enjoying it—as to the rest of us... I suppose Mama revels in his presence." Eliza's gaze drifted across the room, finally resting on Mrs. Bennet and Mr. Collins near one of the fireplaces.

"So you ..."

"I have not yet been driven to distraction. My father has a point to be made when he says 'For what do we live, but to make sport for our neighbors, and laugh at them in our turn?'"

"You cannot truly believe that."

"I can and I must. How else can one endure a guest who follows one around like the oddest little gosling traipsing after a mother goose? Truly, he is at my elbow at every turn. I cannot sneeze lest he offer me a handkerchief."

"Is that not a pleasing solicitude?"

No one had ever paid Charlotte such attentions—and Eliza just dismissed them. Charlotte forced a pleasant smile. Bitterness would not serve anyone well tonight.

"All things in their measure, I suppose. But this is too much." Eliza's shudder started at her shoulders, and coursed all the way down to her toes. "In all seriousness, yesterday he clung like my shadow all day, even watching whilst I sewed. He noted the evenness of my stitches and how his grand patroness favored such industry in young ladies. I have begun to believe, the woman herself possesses no accomplishments apart from critiquing the accomplishments of others!"

"I suppose it is the privilege of the very wealthy to pay others to be accomplished and avoid the trouble themselves."

"If he tells me once more how acceptable I would be to Lady Catherine, I shall—Mr. Collins! Is not Netherfield the perfect image of elegance tonight?" Eliza blushed.

Mr. Collins wove his way through a knot of guests to stand beside Eliza. His round cheeks flushed with the effort of crossing the crowded room. "Cousin Elizabeth, the musicians are gathering. I am here to collect you for the first set."

Hopefully Mr. Collins did not recognize the creases in Eliza's brow for the profound expression of dread that Charlotte knew them to be.

Mr. Long, John's best friend, appeared just behind Mr. Collins. "Have you a partner for the first dance, Miss Lucas?"

"Not yet."

"Will you do me the honor then of dancing with me?"

"Thank you, yes."

They followed Eliza and Mr. Collins to the chalked dance floor. The room was large enough for two lines of dancers. Some care would be required to avoid interfering with the other line's dancers should they be required to cast down the outside of the set. Hopefully, the dances would be carefully chosen and avoid grand moves that could create difficulty for less accomplished dancers.

The musicians played a few opening chords, and Miss Bingley called the dance. Charlotte winced. Perhaps her intention was to point out the weaker dancers amongst them.

Such a maneuver might be acceptable in London, but here in the limited society of Meryton, everyone knew who the accomplished dancers were. The differences did not need to be emphasized so publicly.

Mr. Long was a pleasing partner. Just flirtatious enough to be fun, but not so much as to make anyone wonder at his true intentions. Poor Eliza, her partner proved far less agreeable to her.

Mr. Collins was one of those fellows who struggled to hear the count of the music. Add to that his propensity to confuse right and left, and he made for a mediocre partner at best. Eliza did not help matters with her petulant little huffs and cross looks.

Did she not see how they flustered Mr. Collins and made him lose his place in the dance? Simply knowing his partner's displeasure seemed to shake all other concerns from his mind.

Charlotte held her breath. The next step required Mr. Collins to dance behind the line and back up the center. She grimaced as he nearly collided with Miss Goulding from the next line. He stepped on her hem, and she stumbled to the stomach-clenching sound of fabric tearing.

Eliza rolled her eyes and sighed. No doubt she would pay an apologetic call to Miss Goulding tomorrow. Foolish girl! All Mr. Collins needed were a few gentle cues to remind him of the steps. A few smiles of encouragement would keep him in acceptable rhythm. He had proved a tolerable partner when she had danced with him at the Philips's.

Just because Eliza was quick and clever did not consign the rest of them as insufferable dolts. Did she have any idea, the pride she condemned in Mr. Darcy was as much her failing as it was his?

MARIA GRACE

The set ended and their partners led them off the floor to opposite ends of the room. Another set formed with Eliza and Mr. Darcy near the top. Without a partner, Charlotte wandered the fringes of the rooms, shifting from one conversation to the next with an ease learned by watching Papa in a crowd.

By no means the central topic of conversation, Mr. Collins bore mention more than once. Opinion seemed divided on him. Some found him absurd, others regarded him as quite unobjectionable. Most saw his appointment to Hunsford's vicarage as evidence of his worthiness and good character. Perhaps, it was only his own family that found him so disagreeable.

The music began, Mr. Beveridge's Maggot. How fine Eliza and Mr. Darcy looked together, moving together with elegance and grace. Eliza would be vastly unhappy to know they were by far the smartest couple on the floor. They spoke little, but somehow it seemed entirely right that they should not. Their precisely matched movements spoke all that anyone needed.

Mr. Collins and Mary presented such a painful contrast. Mary danced little and was the worst sort of partner for a man like Mr. Collins. It showed, to the grave discomfort of everyone in their near vicinity. Both turned the wrong way round and lost their place in the steps.

If only Mary had the sense to realize her limitations. She might have arranged for them to take the second couple's role instead of the first. Those simpler steps would have been far more manageable and would have saved them much embarrassment.

Was it truly so difficult to be a considerate partner? Did it require so much? A little forethought and a few quiet requests and so many would be so much more comfortable. Truly no one deserved to endure the stumbling, awkward spectacle Mary and Mr. Collins presented on the dance floor. If only she had been dancing with him instead, and Mary with a more accomplished partner. Everyone would have been so much better off.

At last the horrible set ended, and the dancers retreated. Mr. Collins escorted Mary off the dance floor and found glasses of punch. How would it look if she were to seek out Mr. Collins? His face bore little evidence of his ordeal. Yet, something in the way he held his shoulders suggested he was not wholly insensible.

"My dear Charlotte," Eliza slipped out from behind a tall officer. "I am afraid I must tell you that you were very wrong. I did not find dancing with Mr. Darcy at all agreeable."

"I am surprised you should say that, for your dancing together was most elegant indeed."

"Do not say such things! I would prefer not to think of this again. At least I have no reason to expect Mr. Darcy—"

"Mr. Darcy?" Mr. Collins burst from the crowd and stood a little too close. "How singular that you should be speaking of him. I have found out, by a particular accident, that there is now in the room a near relation of my patroness. None other than the Mr. Darcy of whom you speak. How wonderfully these sorts of things occur! Who would have thought of my meeting with—perhaps—a nephew of Lady Catherine de Bourgh in this assembly! I am most thankful that the discovery is made in time for me to pay my respects to him, which I am now going to do, and trust he will excuse my not having done it before. My total ignorance of the connection must plead my apology."

How his eyes lit at the possibility of a connection to his revered patroness, here so far from home.

Eliza gasped. "You are not going to introduce yourself to Mr. Darcy?"

"Indeed I am. It will be in my power to assure him that her ladyship was quite well yesterday se'nnight."

How singular he should be looking for a service to offer, even on a night like this one.

"Pray sir, I am quite certain Mr. Darcy would consider you addressing him without introduction as an impertinent freedom, rather than a compliment to his aunt."

"Acquainted as I am with the Rosings family I am all but acquainted with him. There is no impertinent informality in such a circumstance."

"There is not the least necessity for any notice on either side. If there were, it must belong to Mr. Darcy, the superior in consequence, to begin the acquaintance. That he has not must imply his wish for privacy."

"My dear Miss Elizabeth, I have the highest opinion in the world of your excellent judgment in all matters within the scope of your understanding. Permit me to say that there must be a wide difference between the established forms of ceremony amongst the laity, and those which regulate the clergy. I consider the clerical office as equal in point of dignity with the highest rank in the kingdom—provided that a proper humility of behavior is at the same time maintained. You must therefore allow me to follow the dictates of my conscience on this occasion."

Eliza stared at him, open mouthed, sputtering and stammering.

"Pardon me for neglecting to profit by your advice, which on every other subject shall be my constant guide. In the case before us I consider myself more fitted by education and habitual study to decide on what is right than a young lady like yourself." He bowed low and left.

How courteous he was in the way he declined her advice.

Eliza covered her face with her hand as he disappeared.

What did she expect? Of course that is what he would do.

Telling someone what not to do rarely dissuaded anyone, especially a determined man. If only Eliza would be willing for a less obvious victory.

All she had to do was to ask Mr. Collins to seek out someone, perhaps, Sir William, who might be able to introduce her to the man related to his revered patroness. A proper introduction would then be made for both of them. How much simpler could it be? Mr. Collins always jumped at the opportunity to serve. What would appeal more that an opportunity to oblige his own sensibilities and hers in one effort?

Instead, Eliza watched with shock and horror evident in her every expression as Mr. Collins exposed himself to Mr. Darcy. At the end of it Mr. Darcy only made him a slight bow, and moved another way.

Mr. Collins returned to Eliza. "I have no reason, I assure you, to be dissatisfied with my reception. Mr. Darcy seemed much pleased with the attention. He answered me with the utmost civility, and even paid me the compliment of saying that he was as well convinced of Lady Catherine's discernment as to be certain she could never bestow a favor unworthily. It was really a very handsome thought. Upon the whole, I am much pleased with him."

Eliza rarely suffered a loss for words. It was not a pleasing sight to see her thus.

"It appears that the dining room is open. Perhaps we should avail ourselves of supper." Charlotte gestured toward the dining room.

"Yes, that is a very good idea. I see Jane, excuse me." Eliza faded into the stream of guests moving toward the dining room.

Mr. Collins's face fell, and he stood, staring at the crowd, a bit lost. Was he so attached to her or the idea of her? It was difficult to discern. Perhaps he did not know himself.

"Supper, Mr. Collins? Are you of a mind to take supper?"

"Ah, oh yes, thank you, Miss Lucas." He craned his neck, probably trying to find Eliza.

"It might be easier for you to find her in the dining room. May I assist you?"

"That is very good of you. I am obliged."

She led him into the dining room. "There she is, sitting near her mother and mine."

"I see no more seats in that part of the room."

"There are several seats in the opposite corner though. I am not Eliza, but if my company would not be too unwelcome, we might sit there."

He bit his lip and continued to scan the crowded room. He was very determined once he got an idea in mind.

"All your cousins are similarly occupied, and you can do no further duty toward them for now."

"I…I believe you are correct, Miss Lucas. Thank you for your hospitality. Where were those seats again?"

"Come, I will show you." Charlotte led him to the corner farthest from any Bennet.

Mama caught her gaze for just a moment and offered a long, slow blink, complemented with a subtle nod. Beside her, Mrs. Bennet huffed and frowned.

They took their seats. Mr. Collins required a bit of coaching, but he soon served her from the nearby dishes and partook himself. Thankfully, his table manners were not wanting. That would have been difficult to discreetly influence.

His eyes remained fixed on the Bennets's side of the room where Mrs. Bennet spoke far too loudly of her expectations.

"Mrs. Bennet seems quite assured of Cousin Jane being settled at Netherfield with Mr. Bingley. The connection appears to give her great pleasure."

"I think most of Meryton is aware of her opinions now," Charlotte whispered.

"I imagine my own connections to the esteemed Lady Catherine de Bourgh should also be very pleasing to her." Mr. Collins turned his gaze to his plate.

How many times had his contributions been overlooked in the past? Next to Mr. Bingley, he must feel much as she did beside Eliza.

When supper concluded someone began the talk of encouraging the ladies to perform. Before Mr. Bingley offered an invitation, Mary Bennet hurried to the pianoforte.

Mary's powers of a weak voice and affected manner were by no means fitted for such a display. Eliza's apparent agonies seemed shared by the Bingley sisters who made signs of derision at each other.

At the end of Mary's second song, with Eliza's less than discreet encouragement, Mr. Bennet rose. "That will do extremely well, child. You have delighted us long enough. Let the other young ladies have time to exhibit."

Charlotte swallowed hard and glanced at Mr. Collins.

"If I were so fortunate as to be able to sing, I should have great pleasure, I am sure, in obliging the company with an air; for I consider music as a very innocent diversion, and perfectly compatible with the profession of a clergyman. I do not mean however to assert that we can be justified in devoting too much of our time to music, for there are certainly other things to be attended to."

He waxed on and on. It seemed as though once he started speaking, he found it impossible to stop despite being uncertain about what to say and unhappy with what he was saying. He kept looking to Eliza and Mr. Darcy as he spoke. With their every wince and grimace he prattled on and on. Only when Mrs. Bennet smiled at him and half-whispered to Mama that he was a remarkably clever, good kind of young man did he find the wherewithal to stop.

Oh, this was so maddening!

Eliza had all but caused this latest debacle. If only she would pay Mr. Collins some attention, give him a few clues on what she wanted. He would be as devoted, and loyal and eager to please as any woman could wish a man to be.

And as for him. What fueled his persistence when she treated him so poorly? Had he no self-respect? Or did dependency and desperation leave him willing to bootlick and grovel for what others would regard as routine courtesy?

If he were that sort of man, the Bennets, any of them, could have him. She had no interest in being dragged into groveling beside him.

As they left from dinner, Mr. Collins hurried to Eliza's side, a puppy dogging after an uninterested master.

Maria bounded up to her, two officers trailing behind her. "Charlotte, you must dance with Lt. Sanderson. He needs a partner for the next set."

"I...I...would be pleased if you would stand up with me, Miss Lucas." Sanderson could not have been much older than Maria, more boy than man.

But dancing with a boy was better than watching Eliza disregarding Mr. Collins as he babbled himself into ignominy.

Lt. Sanderson proved an agreeable partner, with a sense of humor that made up for occasional clumsiness. After their set, he escorted her off the floor. Maria and Lt. Denny swooped in to help him find his next partner.

Eliza caught her gaze and beckoned her come.

Charlotte forced a smile and approached Eliza and Mr. Collins who had moved little since she last saw them.

"You can see, sir, my friend finds dancing very agreeable. I am quite certain she would enjoy dancing the next set," Eliza said.

Was the entire room bent on assigning her partners this evening?

"I mean no offense to your good friend, for I have seen her to be a most agreeable partner. But as to dancing, I am perfectly indifferent to it. My chief object is by delicate attentions to recommend myself to you, my dear cousin. I intend to make a point of remaining close to you the whole of the evening."

Color faded from Eliza's face as she clenched her jaw. "Truly there is no need. I am at no loss for partners in conversation. You would by no means leave me without my share of amusement should you rejoin the dancers."

"How could I answer such consideration and self-sacrifice by leaving your side? I am entirely content here with you."

Eliza's eyes bulged in a silent plea for help.

They were both fools and deserved each other's company for the evening. But Mama would never give her a moment's peace if she left them to each other. If she were to spend the rest of her life with parents or brothers, then best not to have a failure on a night like tonight held over her.

Charlotte drew a deep breath. "Might I join you then? I am too weary to dance another set this evening."

"Oh yes, do." Eliza linked her arm in Charlotte's and pulled her close, her eyes daring Mr. Collins to separate them.

"I would by no means suspend any pleasure of yours, dear cousin. Your delightful friend is a very welcome addition to our little party. Would you ladies like a glass of punch?"

"Yes, yes, that would be excellent," Eliza said.

Mr. Collins bowed, "It is my honor to serve you."

He trundled off.

"Please, please, if you are my friend, stay with me. Do not leave me to endure his ridiculousness alone," Eliza whispered.

"I will stay with you. But you might consider, a little attention from you, a few smiles, and you will find him much less ridiculous."

"How can you say that? If I do as you recommend, who knows what that kind of encouragement might yield? No, no, I must do everything in my power to convince him of my indifference. You must assist me. You provide him the smiles and attention, I beg you."

And continue to receive his indifference? That was indeed cruel.

Then again, he was observant. Perhaps he might notice the difference between them as they stood side-by-side, one ignoring and one encouraging him. Perhaps.

"You need not beg. I am at your service, my friend."

Mr. Collins returned, glasses in hand, and launched into a comparison between the ballroom of Netherfield and that of Rosings. Netherfield, of course, paled by comparison.

Another sort of man would have been rebuffed by Eliza's indifference and might have even noticed the careful attention and encouragement Charlotte provided. But Mr. Collins exhibited a tenacity rarely seen outside a bulldog's kennel.

The musicians played the finishing dance. It was such a merry, fun, and simple dance. Mr. Collins could have done it very well had he a mind to take a partner other than his beloved Eliza. While everything polite and proper, he would not be deterred from the object of his affection.

The dance closed. Papa announced the carriage had been called. A quarter of an hour should be sufficient to see it appear. Though Eliza made clear how much she would repine Charlotte's departure, Mr. Collins seemed indifferent.

Charlotte swallowed back the bitterness burning the back of her throat and excused herself from their company. She had done her duty to her family, and she was done with Mr. Collins, and perhaps with the whole notion of marriage in general. A maiden aunt to care for her brothers' children she would be.

Papa closed the carriage door, and they began their journey home. Papa and her brothers rode on horseback beside them.

"So…" Mama's voice lilted hopefully.

Charlotte closed her eyes and faced the side glass.

"But you spent so much of the evening in his company."

"How did you tolerate him? He cannot dance and his conversation—"

"Maria, stop it. I have no need of your mean opinions," Mama said.

"I found him an agreeable companion, and I believe he thought me agreeable as well. But he is very decided upon Eliza. He would not dance apart from with her or her sisters. He sought no company but hers."

Mama leaned across the coach to pat her knee. "I saw your efforts, my dear, and I am very proud of you."

"I am quite certain he is going to offer for her soon. He is very determined for her. She even tried to make him dance with me tonight and he steadfastly refused."

"So that is why you did not dance with him."

"I do not understand how Eliza can be such a fool!"

"Perhaps her foolishness will yet be to your advantage."

"No, no, it is a hopeless affair. Nothing will dissuade him from her. When she refuses him, he will leave—"

"He made it clear he intends to stay until Saturday." Maria seemed to require her share in the conversation.

"Even if she refuses him tomorrow, it is but another four days. What could happen in that span of time? Especially when he would not even offer me the time of day tonight?" Charlotte clutched the edge of the seat, her voice threatening to crack.

Pray, let no one notice!

"I have invited the Bennets and Mr. Collins to dinner on Friday." She could just make out Mama's self-satisfied smile.

"How could you, Mama? Bad enough that I must give up all hopes of him. Shall I also be forced to watch Eliza –"

"Calm yourself, dear. It is too early for you to give up."

"Too early? No rational creature could look at this situation and believe there is yet any hope." Nor would they want any after seeing the man's foolishness.

"In one of my novels—" Maria said.

"Life is not a novel and I am not romantic, much less a heroine of any kind. Pray just stop. There is nothing more to be said on the matter. Mr. Collins has made his choice… it was not me … and that is for the best." Charlotte let her head fall into the worn squabs.

✤Chapter 4

November 27, 1811

THE NEXT DAY, Maria insisted a visit to the Bennets was absolutely essential. It was simply what was done after a ball. She could not imagine otherwise. What would she do if she could not discuss the officers with Kitty and Lydia?

Though Charlotte's first thought was to refuse, her conscience denied her the luxury. Eliza was still her friend, and nothing about Mr. Collins should change that. So she gathered her bonnet and pelisse and joined Maria on her excursion to Longbourn.

Lydia met them in the vestibule. "I am glad you are come, for there is such fun here! What do you think has happened this morning? Mr. Collins made an offer to Lizzy..."

Charlotte grabbed the back of the nearest hall chair. Though last night she had steeled herself for such news, she hardly expected to be assaulted with it so immediately.

"… and she will not have him."

Kitty bounded into the front hall. "You will never guess what happened."

"You are too late, for I already told them." Lydia wriggled her shoulders in time with her words.

Was she trying to provoke Charlotte to shake her?

"You always share all the exciting news."

"Well, if you were not always such a lay-about you might be the first one sometimes." Lydia sneered.

"Come and join us in the breakfast room." Kitty grabbed Maria's hand and dragged her down the hall.

Mrs. Bennet sat alone in the chamber, woe and vexation written across her face. Granted, it was not an entirely unusual expression for her. "Come in, Miss Lucas, come in."

Charlotte sat near Mrs. Bennet.

"I pray you will have compassion on me, for you—unlike others dwelling under my own roof—are a good and kind girl. I beg you, persuade your friend Lizzy to comply with the wishes of all her family."

"Wishes for what, madam?"

"Why to marry Mr. Collins, of course. What else should she do? It is the right and sensible thing to do. She should be honored by an offer such as his. But the contrary girl is not."

Eliza was indeed contrary. Did Mrs. Bennet believe she could accomplish that which the family could not?

"Pray do, my dear Miss Lucas, for nobody is on my side, nobody takes part with me, I am cruelly used. Nobody feels for my poor nerves."

Jane and Elizabeth appeared at the doorway.

"There she comes," Mrs. Bennet wailed, "looking as unconcerned as may be, and caring not for us. But I tell you what, Miss Lizzy, if you go on refusing every offer of marriage in this way, you will never get a husband at all. I am sure I do not know who is to maintain you when your father is dead. I shall not be able to keep you—and so I warn you. I have done with you from this very day. I told you I should never speak to you again, and you will find me as good as my word. I have no pleasure in talking to undutiful children. Not that I have much pleasure indeed in talking to anybody. People who suffer as I do from nervous complaints can have no great inclination for talking. Nobody can tell what I suffer! But it is always so. Those who do not complain are never pitied."

Charlotte clutched her forehead and turned away. Mrs. Bennet continued her lament. Just how long could she go on? Surely, by her estimation, no one in the history of England had suffered as she.

Mr. Collins entered with a stately air. Where was his distress, his disappointment?

Mrs. Bennet rose. "Now, I do insist upon it, that you, all of you, hold your tongues, and let Mr. Collins and me have a little conversation together."

Elizabeth passed quietly out of the room. Jane and Kitty followed, but Lydia stood her ground. Perhaps she was determined to hear all she could.

Mr. Collins bowed to Charlotte. "How do you do today, Miss Lucas?"

Now he noticed her? How singular.

"Very well, sir, I thank you."

"And your family, are they in good health?"

"I am pleased to report to you they are one and all doing very well today."

"I can scarce imagine better news at this juncture." He glanced over his shoulder at Mrs. Bennet, who pulled the chair next to her out from the table. "Do excuse me."

Charlotte walked to the window and pretended not to listen. Perhaps she should go. If she were a very good girl, she might. But not today. Was it so wrong to hope to hear the condition of Mr. Collins's spirit after suffering rejection? Would he bear it like a man or would he continue his shameless kowtowing? Not that there was much question—

"Oh! Mr. Collins!" Mrs. Bennet said.

"My dear Madam," his voice was curt and sharp, "let us be forever silent on this point. Far be it from me to resent the behavior of your daughter. Resignation to inevitable evils is the duty of us all, especially a young man as fortunate as I have been in early preferment. I trust I am resigned, particularly considering the doubt I feel regarding my positive happiness had my fair cousin honored me with her hand. Resignation is never so perfect as when the blessing denied begins to lose something of its value."

What had he just said? Charlotte clutched the windowsill lest she turn and intrude upon their conversation.

"You will not, I hope, consider me disrespectful to your family, by withdrawing my pretensions to your daughter's favor, without requesting you to interpose your authority in my behalf. My conduct may, I fear, be objectionable in accepting my dismissal from your daughter's lips instead of your own."

"I assure you, sir, her father will yet be prevailed upon to talk sense into her foolish head."

"I have no desire for such intervention, madam. A woman who does not accept me of her own volition is not one I should have offered for in the first place."

Charlotte held her breath. This sounded nothing like the man who trailed like a puppy after Eliza last night, eager for crumbs from her hand. What had happened?

"I certainly meant well through the whole affair. My object has been to secure an amiable companion for myself, with due consideration for the advantage of all your family. If my manner has been at all reprehensible, I beg leave to apologize.'"

"No, no, you have been all politeness and we are very sensible of the consideration you offered."

Mr. Collins buttered a slice of toast and allowed Mrs. Bennet to pour him a cup of tea, beginning her entreaties anew.

Enough of that conversation. Charlotte ducked out in search of the Bennet sisters, finally finding them in the garden. She was welcomed brightly into their company to talk over the ball. Her friends' pleasure was short lived, though, as Mr. Collins joined their number.

One by one, the others slipped off to play lawn bowling and Pall Mall.

"Would you like to join the games?" Charlotte asked.

That would put him again in Eliza's presence.

"As I am good at neither of those sports. I expect I would be a burden on my cousins were I to join. But do not absent yourself from their agreeable company on my account."

"What about a turn about the garden? It is lovely weather for walking and conversation."

"A wholly agreeable pastime." He bowed and gestured toward the garden walk.

They spent the better part of the afternoon in the garden, she listening and he talking. He talked a very great deal, much of it vacuous repetition. Oddly, in none of it did he waffle on about the object of his disappointment. When at last Mr. Collins excused himself to write a very important letter, Eliza immediately took his place.

"You do not know what a friend you are to me Charlotte. You have kept him in good humor the whole of the day. I am more obliged to you than I can express."

"The satisfaction of being useful is one of my chiefest pleasures. It more than makes up for the little sacrifice of time the endeavor has cost."

"Pray consider yourself most welcome to indulge your pleasure again tomorrow. He has two more days with us. I do not know how we shall endure them without your assistance."

"I will do all I can to ensure your comfort."

What better way to assess the truth behind these remarkable, unexpected changes in Mr. Collins?

❧

November 28, 1811

The next day the Bennets were to come and dine at Lucas Lodge. Mama sent Charlotte to Longbourn though, to fulfill Charlotte's promise to Elizabeth. They welcomed her as the bearer of great favor and left her to Mr. Collins for the whole of the day.

To be sure, he could be a bit tiresome. His speeches were long, and he had not mastered the art of give and take in a conversation. His verbosity masked his sense, which was present if one attempted to listen for it. A liberal dose of pride—apparently a trademark of the Bennet clan—colored most of what he said. But what he did not say was most curious of all. He never once mentioned Eliza.

By the time the Bennets departed from Lucas Lodge, she delighted in a bit of quiet to examine her own thoughts.

Mr. Collins was far from perfect, but he was the antithesis of men like Roger, Mr. Bingley and Mr. Wickham. That alone made him appealing. Still, how could she trust a man who turned from attraction to indifference in an instant?

Could she attach herself to a man she dare not trust?

What if he were not as easily led and managed as Mama suggested? She could be trapped with him, unchanged, for the rest of her life.

Was that worse than the fate awaiting her now? Perhaps it was a very good thing that he was to leave on the morrow. Surely Mama would be disappointed, but time would be good for all of them. Perhaps the next time he visited Longbourn she would be more certain—or more desperate. In either case, the choice would not be made in haste.

<hr/>

The next morning, she paced beside her bedroom windows as they caught the morning sun, her thoughts no better settled than they had been the previous evening. What...no, who...was that in the lane? She opened the window and leaned out past the sill. Through the morning mist she just made out Mr. Collins's figure, trundling toward Lucas Lodge.

What could he possibly want this early in the day, far too early for a proper call? She snatched up her bonnet and shawl and scurried down the stairs. Thankfully the squeaky step had been fixed, so no one would be the wiser for her departure.

The morning landscape glowed with a cool mix of pinks and blues, twined with mist and the lingering night air. Her half boots whispered along the gravel, collecting dew upon their nankeen tops. A lovely, peaceful morning, aside from her heart's thundering rhythm in her ears.

"Miss Lucas!" He jumped back.

"Good morning, Mr. Collins."

"I…I…I had not thought to see you here, in the lane, that is to say. Are you in the habit of traversing the countryside so early in the morning?"

"Not usually, sir."

"It is a very peculiar habit, one my Cousin Elizabeth seems to enjoy."

"You have seen her this morning then? Or perhaps you are looking for her?"

"Certainly not." His entire body seems to twitch in revolt. "In truth, Miss Lucas, I came with the purpose of seeking you out."

"Indeed? It is very early for a social call."

"My errand is very urgent, as I must leave at first light on the morrow. Lady Catherine expects me back. I dare not disappoint her."

"Of course, you must do your duty."

He wrung his hands before him, a little sheen of perspiration glistened on his palms. "You have spent a great deal of time in conversation with all of my cousins, particularly Miss Elizabeth. Knowing the propensity for young ladies to indulge in sharing the details of their lives with one another, I am certain you are well aware of my intentions in coming to Hertfordshire. It has always been my design to select a wife from here."

"That was my understanding."

Oh heavens, what he was thinking? Charlotte clasped her hands tightly.

"Although there are many amiable young women in the neighborhood of my parsonage it remains to be told why my views were directed to Longbourn. Being, as I am, to inherit Longbourn after the death of Mr. Bennet, I could not satisfy myself without resolving to choose a wife from among his daughters, that the loss to them might be as little as possible, when that melancholy event takes place."

"So that was your intention, not that of your patroness?"

"To be sure. Twice has she condescended to give me her opinion on this subject. It was but the very Saturday night before I left Hunsford, between our pools at quadrille, while Mrs. Jenkinson was arranging Miss de Bourgh's footstool, that she said, 'Mr. Collins, you must marry. A clergyman like you must marry. Choose properly; choose a gentlewoman for my sake. For your own, let her be an active, useful sort of person, not brought up high, but able to make a small income go a good way. This is my advice. Find such a woman as soon as you can. Bring her to Hunsford, and I will visit her.' But she never advised me to seek out my cousins."

"Then that was your doing alone?"

"For the little effect it had, yes it was. The notion pleased Mrs. Bennet well enough, but as you are well aware, Cousin Elizabeth remained far less impressed."

"I am sorry that you were not able to gain her approbation."

How many men in his circumstance would think to make such a choice, would try so hard to bring it about in spite of the disregard shown him?

"It was a rather shocking disappointment, I confess. Perhaps it is for the best." He clasped his hands behind his back and paced several steps away. "In further consideration, it is entirely likely that her independent and headstrong disposition would not meet Lady Catherine's approval. It would be unwise of me to bring such a woman back to Hunsford."

"I am sorry for the distress you have suffered. It is difficult when a situation turns out so very differently from what one expects."

And confusing…it was very, very confusing.

"I have considered though, that perhaps it is for the best…oh I said that, did I not? Forgive me. I have been deeply torn since the evening we met at the Philips's dinner party. I am a man of decision and purpose, you see. When I decide upon a course, I do not deviate; I must follow it to its natural conclusion. When I arrived in Hertfordshire, I immediately decided upon Cousin Elizabeth as the most appropriate object for my matrimonial intentions. However, almost as soon as I entered the Philips's house, I singled you out as the companion of my future life. But before I am run away with by my feelings on this subject, perhaps it will be advisable for me to state my reasons for marrying—"

"Your feelings?"

He had feelings toward her? The idea swam in her head, muddling her thoughts even further.

"Whilst I pride myself on being a man of sense, I do experience quite violent sensibilities as well. I endeavor not to allow myself to be carried away by the forcefulness of my inclinations; however...perhaps in this case, I have been sorely mistaken."

"I do not take your meaning."

"Since I decided upon my cousin, it behooved me to convince myself that the heated feelings I was experiencing were excited by her and indicative of my right choice. It stands to reason that the feelings should have abated or turned to bitterness at her most vehement refusal of me. They have not. Instead, I have experienced a sharpened clarity, illuminating everything around me."

"And what have you seen?" She had scarce enough breath to form the words.

He paced back toward her. "The real object of my affections has been you. You have been uniformly kind and gracious in every setting, amiable and solicitous toward me. I seek an affable and agreeable partner for life. You are precisely that."

"You know I have even less fortune than Eliza. Can that be acceptable to you or to Lady Catherine?"

"To fortune I am perfectly indifferent. I shall make no demand of that nature on your father, since I am well aware it could not be complied with. On that head, therefore, I shall be uniformly silent. You may assure yourself no ungenerous reproach shall ever pass my lips when we are married. I think it a right thing for every clergyman to do in setting the example of matrimony in his parish."

Was it possible, he preferred her kindness to a fortune?

"And of my person, will your patroness approve?"

"Your kindness and thoughtfulness I think must be acceptable to her, especially when tempered with the silence and respect which her rank will inevitably excite. I cannot imagine that her ladyship would at all disapprove of you. You may be certain that when I have the honor of seeing her again I shall speak in the highest terms of your modesty, economy, and other amiable qualifications. I hope to bring her news that you have accepted my offer."

"Offer?"

"I have allowed my sensibilities to carry me away once again and have never reahed the heart of the matter. Miss Lucas, would you be the companion of my future life, mistress of my home and mother to my children?" He extended his hand.

"You have no feelings for Eliza? The ball…"

He blinked at her, head cocked. "Not at all. At the ball, you saw my determination and strength of decision. Though she engaged my sense, she left my sensibilities untouched."

"You do not repine…"

"It was always my regret to have met you after I had decided my course. I consider it the greatest of fortune than I have been afforded this rare opportunity to follow my inclinations now."

Those were all the right answers. Coming from another, she might not believe their sincerity, but he was incapable of fabricating such fancy. Moreover, he had a comfortable home and wanted an agreeable companion.

He was also pompous, verbose, and apparently very stubborn.

Yet, he responded to her gentle guidance, just as Mama had said.

And above all, he was nothing like Roger.

What more could she ask for?

"Yes, Mr. Collins, I will accept your offer."

He released a heavy breath, color returning to his round cheeks. "You are uniformly charming! Tell me, when, dear Charlotte—I flatter myself to believe myself entitled to call you that now—upon what date shall you make me the happiest of men?"

His 'dear Charlotte'? Gracious that would take some time to become accustomed to. It was excessive to be sure, but entirely in keeping with his character. Not entirely unpleasant, though.

"A date, sir, oh, I hardly know. Would it not be prudent to first apply to my father for his blessings on this enterprise?"

"Of course! You are quite correct. I should have seen it so myself. Already you prove your sound judgment as my helpmeet." He offered her his arm.

"A helpmeet…I like the notion very well." She nestled her fingers in the crook of his elbow.

"I believe that is why Lady Catherine gave me such clear direction in selecting the character of my wife. She well knew…"

Mr. Collins continued on, describing the magnificence of Lady Catherine's condescension, but said nothing to contradict the very key point he had made. Lady Catherine saw his need for a helpmeet to manage and direct him. His patroness would support her efforts to guide and direct him as he should go.

Charlotte would not be alone.

She drew in a deep breath of fresh morning air. No, this would not be an easy path, nor one filled with romantic idylls, but it would suit her very well indeed.

Sweet Ginger

❧ Chapter 1

A Ginger for Mrs. Goddard

THE NEW WOODEN SIGN swayed on its chains, creaking softly in the breeze. Crisp white letters spelled out 'Mrs. Goddard's School for Girls' above the silhouettes of a woman with an open book and a girl looking up at her.

Mrs. Amelia Goddard dusted her hands and smoothed her skirt. Young Jackson had done as good a job as his father had promised after all. She must invite them both to tea soon to thank them.

Now the spring cleaning was done, perhaps she could focus on new things. It had been a long, cruel winter with blizzards, leaking roofs, influenza and septic sore throats. She had never lost a girl in her care before. No amount of cleaning would sweep that memory away, though fresh paint and newly-scrubbed floors helped.

The girls seemed to benefit from the efforts as well. Servants, students and mistress alike shared the hard work of scrubbing, dusting and polishing. Their labors distracted them from their grief and reminded them all of the coming spring.

She always anticipated the advent of spring, but this year, the feeling was particularly poignant. Never had she needed the breath of renewal it brought as much as she did now. She reached into her pocket for the silver comfit box George gave her on their marriage. She removed a ginger comfit.

The children preferred the lemon and mint ones that she kept in the common room jar. But the ginger's sweet-peppery bite appealed much more. It reminded one that sweetness did not exist without sharp, joy without sorrow. Much like her school and her girls.

By and large they were a good lot of children. Some were much loved by their families, some kept conveniently away from older sisters out in society. A few resided with her to be hidden away from society, the natural daughters of men who cared enough to see them provided with decent care.

For a woman with no children of her own, the girls were a joy and a comfort, and a welcome distraction from the sadness that sometimes threatened to overwhelm her. Perhaps if George had lived, they would have had a houseful of their own by now. But fate had not been that kind. All she had left of him was the silver comfit box and a big empty house that cried out in lonely wails each time the wind blew.

George always said, 'Better light a candle than curse the darkness.' He would be proud of the way she had done that. She smiled. Not one candle, but fifteen—fifteen little candles filled her house and her life. Not exactly the way she had planned for it to be, but still, she could be thankful.

Two of the older girls would be leaving her soon, ready to make their come out in society. Amanda Hill, though the same age, would not. If the dear girl were to have any marriage prospects, introductions would have to be arranged in local drawing rooms, parties and perhaps the assembly rooms. Good thing Amanda had cultivated friendships among the local girls. That would be to her distinct advantage.

She pinched the bridge of her nose. Amanda would need new dresses and perhaps a few additional sessions with the dance master. So much to do! She must write to Amanda's guardian right away.

Best get a move on. A new pupil was to arrive today. She ought to wear better than her stained work dress for introductions.

<hr />

Several hours later, while the girls were out with her assistant, Miss Crowe, for their daily ramble, a coach trundled up the lane and stopped before the school. A dusty but well-dressed man descended from the box and handed out a little girl. She wore a plain, drab gown a hand span too long and a poke bonnet far too large for her. They must have been given to her for the journey. The garments appeared good quality, perhaps even new, if ill-fitting. Someone must care about her.

But, no nursemaid or female servant followed her out. Poor dear, traveling all this way with only the dour-looking solicitor for company. He probably required her to be silent and still the entire trip. No wonder she kept her face down, hidden from prying eyes, as she followed him up the path to the front door.

Mrs. Goddard opened the door before he knocked. The child looked frightened enough, no need to keep her waiting at the door, too.

"Mrs. Goddard? I am Mr. Fletcher." The lean solicitor bowed. "This is your new charge." He gestured toward the girl who curtsied, albeit clumsily. At least she had some training in proper behavior.

"Come in, come in." She led them to the parlor and helped the child off with her wrap and bonnet. She had curious, green eyes entirely in keeping with the freckles and red hair that framed them.

The child sniffed. Her pert little nose wrinkled just a mite. "You smell of ginger. Do you like ginger?"

What an odd greeting. "Indeed I do."

A sweet smile broke out on the girl's face. "Oh then I expect you shall like me for I am a ginger, and you like them."

"I am sure I shall, my dear." She patted the girl's shoulder.

"Oh, I do hope so. Not everyone has a taste for ginger. That is what Mrs. Forester told me. She said I must be a very good girl, so good that perhaps you might forget I am a ginger, and then perhaps you might like me."

Oh, the things people were apt say to a child, particularly a sensitive one, like this little mite! Had they no sense? Did they not remember what it was like to be a child themselves? She pressed her eyes with thumb and forefinger.

"Mum, are you well? Mrs. Forester used to do that when she had a headache. Do you have a headache?"

"I am quite well, child, thank you. Why do you not sit here whilst Mr. Fletcher and I speak?" She pointed to a large, soft chair near a small table with several toys.

"Yes, mum." She climbed upon the chair, her feet far from reaching the floor. Her sparkling gaze danced from one side of the room to the other, but her hands remained tightly folded in her lap. "This is a very pretty room, I like it very well. The whole house must be very pretty, too."

Mr. Fletcher walked to a chair and table near the window and placed his hat on the table. "Your school looks just as described in your advertisement, madam. My employer will be most pleased." He sat and leaned back in the chair. His posture could use some attention.

"I am happy to show you the rest of the school if you wish." Mrs. Goddard sat across from him, one eye still on the girl.

"I should like to see it," Harriet said softly.

Mr. Fletcher glowered. "No need to trouble yourself with that, madam. I am entirely satisfied."

And lazy. As he wished, though.

She shrugged. Her standards for her school were probably higher than his or his employers'. She had nothing to hide. "So then as to the arrangements for—" She gestured toward the child.

"Harriet, my name is Harriet," she called from her seat, feet swinging playfully above the floor.

"The arrangements for Harriet—what is her last name?"

Mr. Fletcher dodged her gaze. "Ah—Smith—she is called Miss Smith."

Of course, the poor child was no one's daughter. The signs were all there, but still, she had hoped.

Well, at least little Harriet would be better off here than many of the alternative situations. At least none of the other girls were so high born that they would reject another natural daughter in her care.

She turned to Harriet. "How old are you Miss Smith?"

"I am supposed to be ten years old…no twelve years, mum."

Mr. Fletcher winced.

"Indeed you are. You may play with the toys if you wish."

Harriet smiled. "Thank you ever so much!" She plucked up a set of knucklebones.

Mrs. Goddard pinched her temples and dropped her voice to a whisper. "Did I not make it clear in my letter?"

"You said you would take girls from ten years old and occasionally younger." He folded his arms over his chest.

Naturally, this would not be simple.

"That is the text from my advertisement; however, in my letter to you I believe I made it clear, I did not have room for any younger girls at the moment."

Harriet turned sharply, head cocked toward them. Her smile faded and the sparkle left her eyes. She pressed her lips tightly and swallowed hard.

Pray, let the little dear not cry!

"Perhaps this will help." Fletcher handed her a letter tied with red tape.

She untied it. Gracious, how many banknotes where there?

"The letter contains all you or she need know of her circumstances and my address where you must write with any needs or concerns regarding her. Enclosed you will find full payment for the entire year, including amounts for laundry, an allowance for necessary garments suitable to her station and an allowance for the French, music and dance masters, fee for standing as a parlor boarder, and a bit extra in appreciation for accepting her out of season."

Mrs. Goddard rifled through the banknotes. Yes the amount was exactly as he had said. "It seems her every comfort has been considered."

"My employer desires to see her education is as pleasant as possible. He believes that a contented student will become the most accomplished."

"How generous." And perhaps a touch guilty? At least her benefactor turned his guilt into compassion. Many were not nearly so kind. It boded well for the girl's disposition. Those who knew kindness were often kind themselves. "Where is she to be sent for holidays?"

"Nowhere. She is to remain here. Though, if she makes friends, it will be to your discretion to permit her holiday visits with them."

"How long do you foresee her remaining at my school, assuming of course that I accept her?"

"If all goes well, until she is grown."

Mrs. Goddard pinched the bridge of her nose. Another girl for whom she would be responsible for seeing well settled. Amanda would require so much of her time and effort in the next year, then Hannah and Penelope behind her. How could she take on another? Still it was hard to turn down payment in full and more.

"There is still the matter of her age, sir."

The little girl's face fell, eyes glistening with tears. But she did not pout or slump. She gulped and sat straighter. Dear little thing seemed determined to put on a brave face and make the best of her situation.

Mrs. Goddard beckoned her close. Harriet almost tripped over her too-large shoes in her haste. She caught herself against the settee and made it, breathless, to Mrs. Goddard's side.

"So tell me, child, what have you been taught? What are your accomplishments?"

Harriet wrung her skirt in her hands. "I haven't many, mum, I'm sorry."

Mr. Fletcher harrumphed.

Mrs. Goddard's chest pinched as Harriet dabbed her eyes with her sleeve. "It is all right, child. Just tell me what you have learnt."

"I…I can read a little and…and I can write my letters very pretty with my pencil. I do not know how to use a pen, though." She blinked rapidly.

"What else? Your numbers perhaps?"

"I do not know my numbers so very well, but I know some." She held up her hand. "One, two, three, four, five. Oh, and I learnt to draw just a little. My pictures are very pretty. I can sew and I am very good with little ones. Mrs. Forester keeps four younger than me and a new baby to care for. I dressed and fed and kept them whilst she tended the baby."

Mr. Fletcher leaned forward. "Mrs. Forester did assure me of the girl's excellent disposition despite her limited accomplishments."

Mrs. Goddard sighed. Harriet could not have been more than eight years old, far too young to be sent to school. No, this was not going to work. Perhaps if she had another teacher or even a maid to assist the students. But, with only Miss Crowe there were just not enough hands to attend all their needs. Was it fair to neglect the students she already cared for?

She rubbed her forehead. "I do not know."

Mr. Fletcher removed a wallet from his pocket and added to the pile of banknotes.

The blunt would help, but she needed more than a scullery maid.

"Mum?" Big green eyes blinked up at her. "You like gingers, don't you?"

Oh heavens, those eyes, and the sweet hopeful smile, with dimples like her dear husband had. How she missed them and his smile. Bless it all, George had been a ginger too.

"Yes dear, I do. Bring in her things, Mr. Fletcher. We should get her settled in before supper."

Harriet flung her arms around Mrs. Goddard's neck and kissed her cheek. "Thank you, mum!"

"None of that nonsense now, Miss Smith!" Mr. Fletcher reached for Harriet.

"Leave the child be. She is my charge now." Mrs. Goddard stood and took Harriet by the hand. "Come now. I will show you to your room."

Harriet skipped beside her. Perhaps a little ginger was exactly what her school needed.

❧Chapter 2

THE TIDY, SNUG SCHOOL room at Mrs. Goddard's hummed with students busy at their labors. Harriet hunched over the work table, staring at numbers that steadfastly refused to cooperate.

Why must they be so stubborn? If only they would be obedient and behave like the little girls she minded for Mrs. Goddard! But no, they dare not be sweet like children. They insisted on playing wicked deceitful games with her.

She pushed her workbook away. It was so unfair. Miss Osgood would not permit her to look up answers in the tables of her favorite housekeeping manual.

When—if—she ever needed to sort out servants' wages, how much fabric to purchase to make clothes or how many jars were required for pickles, she would consult the wisdom of Hannah Glasse or Mrs. Rundell who were ever so much cleverer than she would ever be. Is that not why they published books with all that lovely information between their covers?

But then, that would never happen. A girl like her, one with neither family nor connections, and, to make matters, worse, a ginger, would never have an establishment of her own. She straightened her back. It was not all dread and despair. She had a place here, with Mrs. Goddard. This would be her establishment, and her family would be the delightful little girls who flocked to her and loved her. Surely she should rejoice in that.

Miss Osgood walked past and pulled her workbook back to its proper place. She tapped the taunting column of numbers with the end of her pencil. Harriet sighed and knotted her fingers in the soft fringe around her forehead. If she did not puzzle this out soon, she would be sporting a frightful headache the rest of the day.

Two sharp claps rang from the far side of the room. Harriet and the girls around her jumped.

"Your attention, girls." Mrs. Goddard stood in the doorway, a fresh, spotless apron tied around her stout waist, and a crisply-starched cap framing her prim, matronly features.

She stepped inside, two young ladies, probably near Harriet's age and both taller than Mrs. Goddard, followed behind her. Poor dears, they looked a bit timid and definitely uncomfortable being presented in front of so large a group. Had they never been to school before?

What an uncomfortable situation. There must be some way to make them more at ease.

"These are the Miss Martins," Mrs. Goddard stepped back and urged the girls forward a step. "Miss Rachel Martin."

The girl in the grey-blue dress cringed just a little and curtsied. Harriet bit her lip and gripped the edge of her seat. Miss Rachel's cheeks were bright and her gaze toward the floor, clearly uneasy being the center of attention. Every other thing about her seemed bright and cheerful and pleasant.

"And Miss Margaret Martin."

Miss Margaret crushed the skirt of her red calico dress in her fists and attempted a smile. She curtsied, but her face was pale and something like worry creased the corners of her bright eyes.

"They will be joining us as day students for this term." Mrs. Goddard placed a hand on each girl's shoulder as they looked at each other, a little wild-eyed.

New students! How wonderful! Harriet jumped up, clapping softly. "Pray, there is room here. May they sit at my desk with me?"

Mrs. Goddard's eyes shone the way they did when she was pleased. "Indeed they may." She ushered them toward Harriet.

Harriet gathered her books and pencils into a neat little stack, leaving plenty of room for the newcomers.

"I wish all of you to make them feel very welcome. Harriet, if you will make yourself available to introduce them to the other girls."

"Yes, Mrs. Goddard." She curtsied and turned to the new girls. "I am Harriet Smith and am very pleased to make your acquaintance." She smiled as warmly as she knew how. It was the best way to put people at ease. "Pray, sit with me." She sat in the middle of the bench and patted either side.

Miss Rachel sat to her left and Miss Margaret to her right.

"Carry on with your lessons." Mrs. Goddard trundled away.

"You may put away your ciphering for today." Miss Osgood strode to the far corner of the room.

"What a spot of good luck!" Harriet giggled. "I am quite hopeless with numbers."

Margaret pressed her lips together and whispered. "I am as well. Rachel though is quite brilliant with them and always helps me."

Harriet turned to Rachel, hands clasped before her. "Truly? Would you help me with them as well?"

"Well, I..." Rachel stammered. Her cheeks tinged with pink.

Margaret tittered and nudged Harriet. "In return, you must assist her with her sewing. She is dreadful!"

"Surely not!" Harriet. "With such a pretty gown, you must be a very good seamstress."

"No, she is right," Rachel peeked up through beautifully thick lashes and touched the tucks in her bodice. "This is all Margaret's doing. I once sewed sleeves into my brother's shirt without the gussets. He could barely move in it."

"He wore the shirt like that for days before any of us could work out what was wrong." Margaret clapped her hand over her mouth but a giggle still escaped. "I had to pick it all apart and rework it. He was ever so cross with us for making him suffer so with it."

"But then again, he is usually cross about something." Rachel rolled her eyes.

"That is not fair. He is rarely so without reason."

Miss Osgood cleared her throat and cast a sharp look at Harriet. Her tight mouth was a bit of a reprimand to be sure, but her eyes remained soft. "We shall spend the next hour sewing. I have promised the vicar your projects for the parish poor will be done soon. Come up and get your work baskets."

"What shall we do?" Rachel's brow knit, and she cast about the room.

"Do not worry. You may share mine until you bring your own. I have ever so many projects begun, but have such a hard time finishing." She giggled and hurried to collect her basket.

Harriet sat down and the Miss Martins crowded close. Harriet opened her basket and pulled out a jumble of linen. "Here is a baby dress that needs a hem yet. I hate those, they are so boring to sew. Here is a little shirt that needs sleeves, but they are already pinned in. Perhaps that will do for you, Miss Rachel?"

Miss Rachel sniggered and took the shirt. "Only if you will ensure I get it right this time."

"Of course. Perhaps, I should work on these trousers that go with the shirt, that will complete a set. Miss Osgood will like that very much. Miss Margaret, would you work on the baby dress?"

"This looks ever so much like the one I just finished for our little sister. I know exactly what to do!"

They set to sewing, chatting about clothes, and gardens and books. What a very agreeable way to acquaint oneself with new friends.

~❧~

After dinner and a pleasant hour spent playing games in the parlor, Harriet helped Mrs. Goddard tuck the younger girls into bed. Once they were all settled in, Mrs. Goddard left and she read them another chapter from their favorite book of fairy stories. Someday one of them would probably discover that she had changed the ending of ever so many stories.

They might be upset then, but heavens, those tales as they were written were so frightening and disagreeable! How could she not? To be sent to sleep with images of being eaten by wolves, having one's feet cut off to stop dancing or being cooked by a witch? Certainly not her idea of the means to a peaceful rest!

Harriet shuddered. She would risk their displeasure later if it meant they would sleep peacefully and dream pleasantly now. Indeed, several tiny snores confirmed some of them had drifted off even before she had finished.

She tiptoed from the room. Mrs. Goddard stood in the doorway. She had been listening, too.

"You are quite the story teller, my dear. I know for some, this is their favorite time of day." Mrs. Goddard patted her hand.

"They are all so sweet. It is a pleasure. My favorite time, too, I think." Harriet shut the door with a soft click.

"Why do you not go to the parlor whilst I fetch a tea tray for us all."

She withdrew to Mrs. Goddard's parlor where Belinda and Wynne, the other parlor boarders, amused themselves. Belinda sat with a sketchbook and pencil in her lap. She liked to be seen drawing. It made her look quite accomplished, she said. But was it a great accomplishment if her drawings were very poor? They might be better if she did not argue so violently with Miss Crowe's every drawing lesson?

Wynne worked on a piece of fine netting. Elegant, but not terribly useful, or at least it did not seem so. Still Wynne was most proud of it nonetheless.

Harriet sat in her favorite chair, one worn and soft, near the fire. She spread the teaching sampler her future students would learn from over her lap. How pleasing that her guardian had been willing to provide lovely colored silks for her embroidery. The sampler she had been taught from was so drab and boring. The same stitch over and over, all in the same color.

Her students would have something far more interesting to copy. An elaborate floral pattern with each flower boasting different colors and stitches. Not one was alike. True, her students might not be able to afford many colors with which to do theirs, but they would not be bored by repetitive stitches. A very good thing indeed.

"It took you a long time to get the girls settled tonight." Wynne did not look up from her netting. That was nothing unusual. She rarely graced Harriet with a direct look.

"They were still very excited by our new students today." Harriet squinted and threaded her needle. The scarlet twist was so pretty in this light.

"So you coddled them with extra stories—told wrong I am sure—and petting to ensure they will misbehave again." Belinda set her sketchbook aside and pulled herself up very straight in her chair. "You spoil them shockingly, you know."

She liked to think of herself as the head girl at the school. As the eldest student, perhaps she had some right to do so. But it was still most vexing that she thought she knew more about everything than anyone else.

"They were excited, not disobedient. Those are not the same. Besides, it is a pleasing thing for them to be so welcoming to newcomers."

Arguing with Belinda was pointless. She would not stop until everyone said they agreed with her, whether they actually agreed with her or not. Still it was maddening to sit there in silence and allow her to prattle on.

"I hardly find it so." Belinda snorted. "Do you not agree Wynne?"

"Indeed."

Harriet laid her sampler in her lap. "And how do you come to that conclusion?"

"Think about it. To welcome them before we really know their characters, their connections? It seems a very unwise thing to me." Belinda turned her nose up in her favorite oh-so-superior gesture.

Why did she have to do that? She really was not so disagreeable when she was not trying to show off her grand manners and fancy opinions.

"How can you say such a thing? Do you believe Mrs. Goddard would bring unacceptable company into our midst?" Harriet said.

"Have you ever seen her turn away a paying student?" Belinda turned to her with that stare.

The distasteful one, the one designed to remind Harriet that a girl who did not know and might never know her parents, had little place supposing she might know better than one whose father was a successful solicitor and who had an uncle who was a knight or a baronet or something that meant he was called 'Sir'.

Belinda was right after a fashion, though. Harriet really did know very little of the world. All she had was Mrs. Goddard and this school. She lacked the future prospects of so many of the other girls, so she had not bothered to apply herself to much that would not relate to her future, here as a teacher for Mrs. Goddard's school.

She swallowed hard. It would not do to become glum about such things. Mourning what one could never have brought only misery. In truth, she was fortunate. Very fortunate. She was well provided for and had a plan for the future. What more could she want for?

"Has Mrs. Goddard ever taken in a student who proved an unworthy friend?" Harriet asked.

Belinda had no answer.

"Well, I think the Miss Martins were rather plain, drab little things." Wynne turned back to her netting.

"I am sorry to hear you say that." Mrs. Goddard walked in bearing a tray of tea things.

Wynne jumped. "I …I did not mean…"

The cups and saucers on the tray clinked as she set them down. "If you did not mean it, then why did you say it?"

Wynne stammered and muttered something that sounded like "I am sorry, Mrs. Goddard."

"As my oldest girls, it is your duty to welcome visitors and newcomers and help them feel comfortable here. It is a woman's duty to be a warm hostess."

"But that is for her own home, is it not?" Belinda puffed up like a scolding hen.

"This is currently your home, and may be for quite some time yet. If you cannot make guests welcome here, how will you do so elsewhere?"

Belinda tossed her head. She obviously missed Mrs. Goddard's sharp warning look.

Harriet cringed a little. "I thought them very sweet and agreeable girls."

Wynne rolled her eyes like she always did when Harriet spoke.

That was something else of which Mrs. Goddard did not approve. Perhaps neither of them minded a scolding as much as Harriet did.

"And they and I were very pleased at the way you dedicated yourself to their comfort, my dear." Mrs. Goddard handed Harriet a cup of tea.

"But their manners! You cannot say they were at all polished or even that proper." Belinda reached for a cup.

"Perhaps they are in need of a bit of polish, but is not that what school is for?" Mrs. Goddard extended a plate of biscuits. "They are very eager to learn, to be sure. They desire to be a credit to their brother."

"Who is their brother?" Belinda was always interested in young men, particularly if they might have property.

"Mr. Robert Martin of Abbey Mills Farm. He is a very respectable young man with a very pretty establishment."

"I imagine Mrs. Martin is a very pretty and respectable wife?" Wynne snickered behind her hand.

"The only Mrs. Martin is their mother." Mrs. Goddard added sugar to her tea.

"Oh." Something in Belinda's voice changed as it trailed off. She chewed her lip and little furrows appeared between her brows. "Has my father written to you yet—"

"About preparing you to come out? Yes he has." Mrs. Goddard leaned back and sipped her tea. Everything in her posture declared she was most tired of the subject. "He said that you should be allowed to attend small gatherings in private homes that I deem acceptable to continue your preparations."

Belinda clapped softly. "Capital! I am so glad he did as he promised."

Botheration. Belinda had that look in her eyes, the one that meant she was planning how to make others pleased to give her what she wanted. The one that made Harriet avoid her wherever possible.

On the positive side though, perhaps Belinda would be nicer to the Miss Martins now.

<hr/>

The next morning, Harriet was helping the younger girls with their lessons when the Miss Martins arrived. They waved at Harriet.

Belinda and Wynne made space on their bench for them and beckoned them over.

Rachel and Margaret whispered to each other for a moment, then sat with Belinda and Wynne as Miss Osgood continued her geography drill.

What a horrid subject, geography. How boring to recall what strange names went with what little squiggly colored patch on the globe. What use was it to know such things when she would never see any of those places herself nor know anyone who would? Far more interesting was learning the plants in the garden and which would soothe the stomach aches and colds the change of seasons would inevitably bring.

As well, at least if she had to study geography, she had her fair share of more interesting subjects as well. Even better, she could skip the lesson altogether today whilst helping the little ones with their penmanship.

She bent over one of the youngest girls' desk to help her hold her pen correctly.

"Be sure to copy that maxim correctly." Harriet tapped the copy book. "Remember, where there are two 's's together, the first is always a long one. Keep practicing and I am sure Miss Osgood will soon find you ready to do a writing blank to send to your father and mother."

"I do hope so, Miss Smith. I already know the one I want to use, and I have picked out the verse to write as well."

"Is Miss Smith a teacher here too?" Rachel whispered.

Harriet glanced at them from the corner of her eye.

"Not yet, but almost as good as one." Belinda replied, eyes fixed on the map she drew. "She is set to work here after the next term. You can see she is practicing now and is very good with the younger students."

"But why—"

"She has no ... connections you know, and is the natural daughter of, well no one knows who."

Harriet's cheeks burned and she screwed her eyes shut. What place did Belinda have mentioning that when it need not be said? Just because her father was a very successful solicitor—

"Miss Smith?" A small face looked up at her.

Oh bother! Harriet still held the little girl's hand in hers. "Like this dear. Try the long 's' again."

She murmured something and returned to writing an awkward row of long 's's in running hand across her paper.

"I had no idea," Miss Margaret whispered, with a sidelong look at Harriet.

Miss Rachel leaned a little closer to Belinda. "She is such a nice girl."

"She is nice and proper. She knows her place among her betters and that is a very desirable thing in a young lady. Her manners do her much credit." Belinda started to bat her eyes at Harriet, but Miss Osgood's sharp look stopped her.

Even Harriet could tell Belinda spoke what she did not mean. "Continue your practice. I will return in a moment." She tapped the desk and darted out.

Once in the hall, she increased her pace to nearly a run until she escaped into the gardens. She gulped the soft air like a drowning man, but relief for her true need was not to be found. She ran for a cluster of trees, pushing herself until her sides ached and throat burned.

But running only moved the pain temporarily from her heart to her body. She could not run fast or far enough to escape the truth of who she was—and was not.

This was not the first time Belinda had reminded the other girls of Harriet's pitiable state. Belinda was so conscious of status and rank! She loved to remind others of it and, it seemed, drew them to her like moths to a glittering flame.

Sometimes it worked, and they treated Harriet coolly for a time, but sometimes it did not. It only made Belinda try harder. Could she not see that was not the way to attract real friends?

Harriet was far from friendless—in truth, she probably had more friends than Belinda. That made Belinda jealous, or so Mrs. Goddard said. She insisted Harriet should feel pity for Belinda's antics, not anger.

Perhaps that was true. But it did not change the hurt plaguing her each time Belinda played her maneuvering games.

"Harriet? Harriet?" Mrs. Goddard called, her voice distant, probably at the edge of the trees.

"Here, madam." Harriet dried her eyes with the edge of her chemisette's high collar and hurried toward the voice.

"Are you well child? The maid saw you run out and told me straight away." Mrs. Goddard met her at the edge of the copse.

"I am fine, truly."

"No, my dear you are not." She took Harriet's hand. "I have seen you wear that expression far too many times."

"It is nothing. Only one of my flights of fancy grabbing hold of me once again. You know how I can be, dashing here and there after a stray idea. I should be getting back to the school room." Harriet tried to pull away, but Mrs. Goddard's kind grasp remained firm.

"Do not lie to me child. I know you far too well for that. Do you not know by now?"

"Yes, Mrs. Goddard." She tried to hide her sigh in an ineffectual little smile. It was so difficult not to look fretful when one felt so.

"Come now. Sit with me in the gazebo and tell me what happened."

Mrs. Goddard led her along the garden path to the little white gazebo surrounded by heather and covered with ivy. It slanted to the left a bit and a few vines drooped inside, but that only added character, making it her favorite spot.

"I am being foolish and petty." Harriet mumbled, eyes fixed on a particular clump of heather that needed trimming. The soft green smells and the cool shade soothed the ragged edges of her spirit. This place always made the ache inside subside.

It never really left, but it was made bearable here.

"Belinda?"

Harriet shook her head in something that meant neither yes nor no. It satisfied most people enough that they asked nothing more.

"She continues to remind you—"

"Of what is the way of the world." Harriet paced along the viney walls. "It is not cruelty. Only truth. I cannot, I should not hide from it. I am … am old enough to accept it for what it is and not sulk like a little girl. I have so much to be grateful for. I must never lose sight of it."

"You are right, child, that is what you must always focus upon. There are enough troubles and hardships to convince us to be sad. But that is not to say we cannot make efforts to better ourselves and our situations."

"I do not know what you mean."

"I know you must be a little envious of Belinda's planned come-out."

"It is a very bad thing to be jealous. I do not wish to feel so."

"True enough. But still, it does suggest I have been remiss and selfish." Mrs. Goddard stood and dusted her skirts like she did when she was about to start to work.

"How can you say that?"

"I have been far too content in the idea of keeping you with me always. You are like a daughter to me. I have taken comfort in the thought of always having you close."

A warm spot tingled in Harriet's chest. "And I have always thought of you as a mother more than a school mistress."

"Then it is time for me to act as a mother should. Your guardian has given me full leave to handle your education as I see fit. I believe it is time to introduce you into society."

"Me? But…but I am not … not …"

"While it is true, there are those who might not accept you for reasons well beyond our control, I am quite certain there are those who are willing to look beyond such things to the very agreeable girl that you are. I will make it my purpose to discover them and see you are introduced."

"But truly, I am content…"

"You think yourself content because you know you should be. I know you better than you yourself do. You want what every young woman desires. A home and a family of your own. I will see you have that. But you must trust me and do as I tell you."

"Have I not always done so?"

"Yes, you are a very good girl. You deserve your measure of happiness. I will see you have a chance for it. For now though, come, let us return before the little ones become unruly without you."

They walked back to the house.

What would it be like having a home of her own? It never seemed possible. What an odd…and very pleasing thought. But very, very unlikely.

❧ Chapter 3

FOR THE NEXT SEVERAL DAYS, Harriet kept to the younger girls, leaving the Miss Martins to enjoy the wonder of Belinda and Wynne's company. It seemed the feeling was entirely mutual. In the parlor after dinner, Belinda gushed about the pleasures of her new friends and how she expected to soon secure an invitation to their house for dinner.

"Ooo! A dinner invitation!" Wynne clapped. "That would be so delightful. I think it a very nice way to practice for your coming out. Don't you agree, Harriet?"

"Mind your diction, Wynne, a proper young lady does not slur her words together in unseemly ways." Mrs. Goddard did not look up from her knitting. If anything, her needles clacked together more rapidly.

How funny that her knitting needles could so clearly reflect her moods.

"Yes, Mrs. Goddard. Still, I do think it would be very nice." Wynne plucked at a stubborn stitch gone awry.

"I should like it very much. I might even be invited to spend the night when they see how entertaining I am." Belinda pretended to sketch a little still life she had spent a great deal of effort arranging on a small table near the fireplace. Artistic though it might be, feathers, fruit and books did not seem to belong together.

"Perhaps your expectations are a bit too high." Mrs. Goddard did not look up from her work.

"Too high? Whatever do you mean? Have you not seen what a very gay time we have together?"

To be sure, Belinda seemed to enjoy their company very much. But, if she thought about it very much, Rachel and Margaret did appear a touch less satisfied.

"Have you considered that perhaps your father might not wished you connected with a family of farmers? Your society is a little high for that, is it not?" Mrs. Goddard's eyebrow rose just so.

Was she making a joke, or was she serious? It was an odd thing to say. Humor was so difficult to make out sometimes. Harriet bit her lip just in case. It was very poor manners to laugh when one should not.

"I do not know. Perhaps that might be true. I do not regard such things though, at least not very much. They are very agreeable girls."

"With a brother considered a rather eligible match in some circles."

"Indeed? I had not given that a second thought." Belinda flicked her long elegant fingers.

"I am pleased to hear it. Your father would not wish to see you entertaining suitors from Highbury."

"I am not looking for a suitor, madam."

Belinda would have been more convincing if the corner of her mouth had not drawn up and her eyebrow twitched.

"I am pleased to hear it."

Wynne covered her mouth and giggled. "But flirtations are an entirely different matter."

"Wynne!" Belinda jumped up so fast she knocked her still life apart. A wooden bowl tumbled to the floor and rolled onto Mrs. Goddard's foot. "Look what you have made me do!"

Mrs. Goddard picked up the bowl and walked to Belinda. "I need not to remind you, any of you, that I do not approve of flirtations. They are unseemly and dangerous to a young woman's reputation."

"Yes, Mrs. Goddard," they all intoned together.

Mrs. Goddard removed her glasses and pinched the bridge of her nose.

"Shall I clean your glasses for you?" Harriet reached for them. "Smudges always give you headaches."

"Thank you dear." Mrs. Goddard handed her the glasses.

Wynne rolled her eyes and Belinda smirked. Harriet clenched her jaw. Why did they always do that when she spoke? Did they not realize it was hurtful and rude? Still, it was not her place to correct them. But she would make a point to ensure the little ones did not ape their disagreeable habit.

***

The Miss Martins attended every day for the next several weeks. Though usually in the company of Belinda and Wynne, sometimes when the girls took their daily walks, they would break away and walk with Harriet.

Those were jolly times indeed. They discussed the chapters they read of Romance of the Forest as they passed the book between themselves. Margaret had a truly wicked sense of humor as she parodied the characters. Rachel's astonishing memory allowed her to repeat lines from the book for Margaret to play against. How they laughed and laughed. Though Harriet had relished many friendships, the Miss Martins were by far the finest company she had ever enjoyed.

When she had the rare opportunity to enjoy it.

More often, she watched from the other side of the room as Wynne and Belinda fawned over Rachel and Margaret. She probably could have joined them, had she been of a mind to—of a mind and a stronger constitution. Belinda and Wynne would not dare tell her she was not welcome with them. Still, they had a way of letting her know when her company was appreciated and when it was not. When the Miss Martins were there, it definitely was not.

<hr />

One cold and rainy morning, Harriet paced the front hall. The Miss Martins had not yet arrived and with weather so bad, it was difficult not to worry. Mrs. Goddard insisted they would not come today. It was only sensible that young ladies would not walk out in the rain. But, it was just possible that they might, so Harriet begged leave to watch for them. And just in case, she made certain a welcoming fire crackled in the morning room and dry towels warmed in the kitchen.

A heavy fist pounded on the front door.

Harriet scurried to open it. A broad-shouldered man in a sodden great coat and hat stood beside a half-drowned looking Margaret.

"Pray do come in. Quickly now, you are soaked to the skin." Harriet took Margaret's pelisse and the man's very heavy coat.

"This is my brother, Mr. Robert Martin," Margaret barely got the words out through chattering teeth. "I am very cold…"

"You would not be, had you not insisted in venturing out in this weather." Mr. Martin removed his hat. Rivulets poured off and puddled on the floor.

"Come to the fire. I will fetch some towels." Harriet directed them to the morning room and hurried to the kitchen, pausing briefly to tell Mrs. Goddard of Margaret's state.

She returned, arms piled with towels and stopped short just outside the morning room.

"Margaret dear, we were all so worried about you. I am so relieved to see you, though perhaps it would have been better for you to stay at home." Belinda glanced up at Mr. Martin.

"I am glad to hear they teach sense at this academy." He slicked water off his cheeks with his palms.

Harriet swallowed back her sigh. Perhaps she should let Belinda tend to their needs. But it was not fair to them to force them to wait, cold and wet, until she noticed their requirements. Harriet slipped inside.

"This might be better suited to the task." Harriet handed him a warm towel.

He took it from her hand, his eyebrow raised. Was he not accustomed to warm towels? Harriet draped a towel around Margaret's shoulders.

Margaret clutched the towel around her, shivering.

"Stand a little closer to the fire." Harriet guided her forward.

"No, no, you do not want her dress to catch fire." Belinda grabbed Margaret's elbow.

"As damp as she is, I think there is little danger of that." Mr. Martin harrumphed and stepped a little nearer himself.

Margaret slipped Harriet a sidelong glance and giggled.

"Well you are here, now, Margaret. I shall be about my business now." Mr. Martin glanced about the room, presumably for his coat.

"What business could you have on a day like this? Surely you would be better served warming yourself by the fire and staving off a nasty cold." Belinda gestured to a chair.

He glared down his nose. "A farmer does not last long if he is gainsaid by weather such as this."

Harriet retrieved his coat from the stand in the front hall. "Here, sir. But first," she held out several warm towels. "Your comfort would be increased if you put these under your coat."

Belinda snorted.

Mr. Martin laid the towels over his shoulders, a funny little crook to his lips. "You are most kind Miss…"

"Miss Smith, my friend Harriet Smith." Margaret's shivers had nearly stopped.

"Mr. Martin," Mrs. Goddard bustled in with a tray of hot spiced apple juice. "If you cannot stay, pray, at least have this before you leave." She handed him a mug.

"Ah…thank you." He took it from her as though uncertain what exactly to do with it.

Poor man, he was definitely not at ease in company. Much like his sisters and some of the little girls when they first came to Mrs. Goddard. Sometimes it took them time to adjust and some gentle help understanding how to be acceptable in company. How strange to think a grown man might feel very much the same.

He drank it down quickly enough to be considered rude. Belinda sneered a dainty little smirk behind her hand. She never liked to make allowances for anything even slightly improper.

"Thank you." He handed Harriet the mug and hurried away, Mrs. Goddard following close behind.

Harriet gave Margaret another towel and helped her take down her hair. She rubbed it with the towel.

"Where is Rachel this morning?"

"She slipped in the mud just a bit from the house and turned her ankle. She could not walk all the way here on it."

"I am very sorry to hear that. I looked forward to discussing chapter five with her. The story takes a most surprising turn."

"Oh, I know, what did you think when—"

"I am surprised you did not drive here in your carriage," Belinda murmured.

"We only have a gig and the hood is not yet mended. It is not very good for wet days. The wheels get stuck in the mud."

"But your good brother intends to remedy that soon, I am sure." Belinda patted her hand. "You poor dear, soaked to the skin. You cannot remain in your wet garments! Harriet, how could you insist on such a thing? It is too cruel."

Harriet sputtered something unintelligible.

"You must come up to my room and borrow one of my dresses to wear whilst yours dries."

"That is a very good thought." Mrs. Goddard said. "But I think Harriet is much more her size. Harriet, take Margaret upstairs and loan her a gown. Bring her wet things to dry in the kitchen."

"Yes, Mrs. Goddard."

Margaret grabbed Harriet's arm and dashed upstairs. "Oh, thank you! I was afraid Belinda would force me to use one of hers and leave me beholden to her."

Harriet led Margaret to her cozy little room under the gable. "Why would she do such a thing? I am sure she was just concerned for your health. It is not good for you to be so cold and wet. I am sorry I did not think of it first."

"You are far too kind and sweet for your own good. Harriet. Cannot you see Belinda wants to wrest a dinner invitation from us?"

"No, the thought had not crossed my mind at all." Perhaps that was a small fabrication. "Here, do you like this dress, or would you rather this one?"

"They are both very pretty—I do not know. You pick."

"Well this one is my favorite, so I should be happy to see it on you."

Margaret slipped off her sodden gown. "You see that is the difference between you and Belinda. You would happily lend me your favorite gown and never say a word of it to anyone. Belinda would force a gown she did not favor upon me and crow to the world of the kindness she bestowed. All the while reminding me of how very fine her gown was and how much I must enjoy wearing it."

"You do not like Belinda very much, do you?"

Margaret sniggered. "Not really. You had not noticed?"

"I thought you very fond of her—you and Rachel both."

"Why ever would you think such a thing?"

Harriet blushed and turned away to find Margaret some dry body linens and stockings.

"Oh, Harriet!" Margaret touched her shoulder. "We have hurt your feelings spending so much time in Belinda's company."

"No, no, not at all. It is quite right for you to spend time with anyone you like."

"But not when it leaves you to believe you are not our dear friend."

"Truly it is nothing. Pray do not be concerned."

"I am, though. Belinda is haughty, self-important and cunning. I do not like to be used. She seeks to manipulate Rachel and me to her own ends. We just have not figured out a way to wrest ourselves away from her. She is so very persistent."

"She is that."

"Pray, forgive me—forgive us if you have felt in any way slighted. We would much rather have your company than hers."

Harriet blinked rapidly. What a very kind thing to say, although Belinda would not appreciate hearing so. "I do enjoy keeping company with you and your sister very dearly."

"Then say you will come home with me for dinner tonight."

"But your mother—"

"She asked me to extend the invitation. She thought it would cheer Rachel's spirit very much. She already expects you tonight. My brother agreed as well, though he was grumpy about it as he usually is. Say you will come, please."

"I must ask Mrs. Goddard's permission, but if she consents, I should be very happy to have dinner with you tonight."

"How wonderful! I am sure he already spoke to her about it. Hurry and help me dress so we may ask her directly!"

Margaret dragged Harriet, wet garments in hand, downstairs. Margaret dashed off in search of Mrs. Goddard while Harriet made her way to the kitchen. Cook directed her to set a drying rack by the fire, perhaps two, as she expected more before the day was out.

Harriet piled the wet things on the large table and wrestled the drying racks from their spot in the pantry. Mrs. Goddard usually had the wash sent out so they were not needed but for the odd bit or two in rainy weather. Though she was exceedingly grateful not to have to do laundry herself, the distinct disadvantage now was that she found herself at odds with the awkward racks. Lightweight, but ungainly at the best of times, there was a particular knack to setting them up, one which she had never acquired. The seemed much like the puzzles she was so very bad at solving.

"How can you be so dumb, yet clever enough to obtain an invitation from the Martins?" Belinda stood in the kitchen doorway, hands planted on her hips.

"I do not know what you are talking about." Harriet smacked her ankle with the corner of the rack.

"Of course you do not." Belinda flounced in and circled Harriet. "You are far too simple to understand much of anything. I cannot fathom why Mrs. Goddard would want you as a teacher."

It was true. Or at least it seemed so very often. She was a fright at ciphers and geography always left her confused. But she could read and knew her gardening and her needlework and handwriting were always praised. She could sing very prettily and write a very proper letter…

"You do not even understand what I said." Belinda stopped in front of the fireplace.

Poor Belinda. She always got this way when she was jealous or angry. It happened regularly enough. Such little things seemed to vex her. It would not do to add to it, though one day it might be very satisfying to speak her mind, just once.

"I need to dry Margaret's dress, and you are standing in the way of the drying rack."

"And what are you going to about it?" Belinda folder her arms across her chest.

One never won an argument when Belinda was in this temper. Harriet shrugged, pressed one drying rack at Belinda and gathered the other under her arm. "Cook said to set this up by the fire." She retrieved the clothes from the table and picked her way to the morning room.

"Harriet?" Mrs. Goddard's voice had an edge of irritation, but it was not nearly so irritated as it would soon be. "I told you to dry those in the kitchen."

Harriet handed the pile of wet things to Margaret who just stared at her.

"There was no room by the fire." Harriet edged around Mrs. Goddard and set up the drying rack.

Fickle thing now chose to behave quite properly.

"No room? Whatever are you talking about?"

"Belinda may be better able to answer than I."

Margaret giggled.

No doubt Mrs. Goddard rolled her eyes. It was her most common response to Belinda.

"I see. Never mind then." Mrs. Goddard helped Harriet lay the wet garments over the rack. "Margaret has asked for you to visit for dinner tonight and I have given my permission."

Margaret squealed and clapped softly.

Harriet draped the last stocking to dry and curtsied. "Thank you very much, madam."

"Margaret, go up to the school room and begin your lessons. I will send Harriet up directly."

"Yes, madam," Margaret dipped in a quick curtsey and scurried out.

Mrs. Goddard followed her and shut the door.

Oh gracious, was Mrs. Goddard far more upset about Belinda than usual? Harriet's neck prickled. It was awful when Mrs. Goddard scolded.

"You may relax, dear. I am not at all upset with you."

Harriet exhaled heavily. "Pray, do not be too angry with Belinda. She does not know how to manage envy. I am sure she would like to behave more properly…"

"You do not need to explain her to me. I understand her very well, my dear. You forget just how long I have been keeping young ladies in my school."

"Forgive me, I just do not like seeing you disquieted."

Mrs. Goddard patted Harriet's hand. "You are very thoughtful of me, child. I am pleased Margaret invited you. Come here, sit by me." She sat on the couch and pointed to the cushion beside her.

Why did Mrs. Goddard look so serious? Harriet sat beside her and peered into her face.

"Do you recall the afternoon we talked in the gazebo?"

"I do."

"I told you then it was my purpose to see you introduced into society?"

"Yes."

"Girls typically prepare to come out by attending small gatherings in homes, with family and old friends. That is what you will do tonight."

"You mean I am coming out?"

"Not precisely, not yet. But you are preparing for it, practicing, shall we say. The Martins are good people, even considering Mr. Martin's manners are less than polished. He is most solicitous of his sister's' happiness and reputations. He will guard yours as well. So if the evening is…ah…less than perfect, there will be no unkind talk."

"You are afraid I will embarrass you?" Harriet stared at her hands and rubbed them together in her lap.

"No, I never said that."

"But you are concerned I will say or do something—"

"I would not send you out if I was not absolutely certain of you. But, I remember my first time in company and it was not without its difficult moments. In case that happens to you, I want to make sure you are with those who will be kind."

"Oh." That did not sound so bad.

"What is more, I have the greatest trust in you that you shall be properly behaved in company not coquettish with Mr. Martin. He is a good man, but it is well known in town that he is not yet in a position to marry. He is supporting his mother and brother and sisters. Any kind of flirtation with him would be unseemly and unwelcome." Mrs. Goddard chewed her lower lip. "He does not make you nervous with all his gruff manner and dour looks does he?"

"No, not at all. He was not at all disagreeable. What else does one expect someone to be when cold and wet and in need of going out further in such distasteful weather."

Mrs. Goddard chuckled and shook her head. "Only you would say, or even think such a thing. You shall have a very pleasant time with your friends tonight."

"I do hope so, and look," she pointed to the window, "it even looks like the rain is tapering off. Perhaps by tonight it will have ceased altogether."

"You always do seem to see the bright side of things, my dear. Highbury may not be very much, but it is likely the only society you will have the opportunity to experience. I will see you have the chance to know it and be known by it. I hope to introduce you to more friends like the Martins. I shall promote you as any mother promotes her daughter. Nothing may come of it, but then again, it may."

Mrs. Goddard had such hopes for her. But such dreams were frightening things with their power to hurt if they did not come to pass. "I should like to meet new friends, I think. I am sure they are many agreeable girls in Highbury."

Mrs. Goddard kissed her cheek. "Yes, there are and I shall make a way for you to meet as many of them as possible, beginning with the Martins. That is the best hope we have of seeing you mistress of your own establishment someday."

What a frightening thought, fearful and delightful both. Could she even manage such a task should it come her way? Mrs. Goddard seemed certain of it and she had never misled Harriet. Maybe, just maybe…oh, it would be very, very pleasing to be able to have children of her own one day.

Chapter 4

HARRIET CLIMBED THE STAIRS one step at a time, lingering, like a little girl still unsteady on her feet. What would it be like to teach a child of her own to scale the mountain of stairs? There had been one little girl, Abby, who had been so frightened of them! It took months of holding her hand before she was willing to do them on her own. Dear, silly little thing.

"Oh! Watch where you are going!" Belinda dodged around her.

"Oh I am sorry." Harriet clung to the railing, pressing against the wall.

"Gathering wool again, I suppose."

Harriet regained her footing and pulled herself up straight.

"I would not get my hopes up if I were you." Belinda wrinkled her nose in her favorite little sneer.

"My hopes of what?"

MARIA GRACE

"Truly you can be such a dullard. You know very well what I mean, Of Mr. Martin or of ever getting away from this drab little school."

"What do you mean of Mr. Martin? Margaret and Rachel are my friends. I am going to visit them. What has he to do with it?"

"You truly are very simple. Did you not consider that he is unmarried?"

"No, I did not give it much thought. Why would I?"

"And that is exactly why you will never leave this place. How will you get a husband if you do not even try to look for one?"

"You do not need to be jealous. Mrs. Goddard said he is not in a position to marry now. You are missing nothing by not getting to meet him." Harriet touched her arm, but she snatched it away.

"Why would you think I would want to meet him? A farmer who does not even own his farm is not the kind of husband I want."

"Good, then you have nothing to repine."

Why did she not look happier about it?

"I suppose he is just the sort of man who would not object to your kind as a wife, even if you are a ginger."

Ah yes, her kind. Harriet tucked stray hairs behind her ear. A little seed of bitterness heated in her belly. No, she was not likely to ever forget all that made her undesirable. "Good that he is not looking for one, then." She pushed past Belinda and hurried up stairs.

At the top, Harriet turned away from the school room and ducked into the maid's closet. Back against the door she pressed her hands to her stomach and gulped cool air to staunch the growing heat within.

Dwelling on what she could not change achieved nothing. It never had and it never would. She had friends, good friends, a home and a future here with Mrs. Goddard no matter what else happened. That was more than so many had.

It was just a dinner with friends, not presentation before the king. Her future did not depend upon her making a proper curtsey or conversing smartly with peers. She could have a merry time and ensure those around her happy she had been invited. Surely she could.

What was the worst that could happen? If she failed, she might never have another invitation and Mrs. Goddard might abandon the idea of introducing her into Highbury society. All would go back as she knew and expected. That would not be so bad.

But then, she might never have a little girl to teach to climb steps.

There would always be students at the school though, and that would be enough. It would have to be.

Miss Osgood set Harriet to helping the little girls with their samplers. It was unfortunate that the pattern was so dull, though. Miss Osgood had little imagination and a high tolerance for repetition, it seemed, given how many times the same motif appeared in her work. The girls seemed content enough to stitch it, though. The quiet familiarity of sitting and sewing with them calmed Harriet's spirits and passed the afternoon quickly.

The rain stopped just before evening. The clouds parted just enough to permit a few feeble rays of sun to kiss the ground. Mrs. Goddard suggested they leave now, before the fickle weather shifted again. She bundled up Margaret's now dry, but very wrinkled things and pressed them into Harriet's hands on their way out the door.

"I wish she had allowed me to change back into my own clothes." Margaret kilted up the skirt of Harriet's dress. "I do not want to get mud on your favorite dress."

"Do not be so concerned. It will wash you know."

"It seems like a very ill way to use what you have lent me."

"I offered you a dress on a rainy wet day. Even I might perceive the possibility of it getting muddy."

They laughed and linked arms.

Margaret pressed her head to Harriet's shoulder. "You are so funny. I think my mother shall like you very well indeed."

"Oh," Harriet paused, nearly causing Margaret to stumble. "I had not thought of that."

"Of what?"

"That she might not like me very well. You have often called your brother grumpy, so I thought it possible he would not. What if your mother does not?"

"Why would you think that?"

"Did you not just say—"

"That she would like you very much."

"But what if—"

"Enough fretting. I know she will." Margaret pulled her forward and peered at Harriet from the corner of her eye. "You have not met many people, have you?"

"Only students at the school." Harriet pressed her toes into the squishy black mud.

"That is unfortunate. Meeting new people is great fun. But, I am pleased the rest of my family shall be the first of your acquaintances."

"Rest of your family?" How many are there?"

"My mother and brother, you know of them. Rachel and me, then there are my four little sisters and a younger brother."

"Eight of you? That is a fine, large family." What must it be like to have such a family? So many connections, all together in one home.

"Large and loud and lively I am afraid. We have no governess and my younger brother and sisters are…" Margaret turned aside, a hint of crimson on her cheeks.

"All very dear I am sure. You are so very lucky to have so many people."

"You may not feel that way after you have met them all. My mother considers my sisters more than she is up to on many days. That is why she was reluctant to send us to school. She wanted our help at home with them."

"I feel much better knowing you have so many little ones at home. I am ever so fond of children."

"I had hoped so. You seem so well pleased with them at school. Not everyone is fond of seeing and hearing children they consider belong in their nursery, away from polite company."

Harriet giggled. "No one has ever considered me polite company. I do not think anyone has ever considered me for company at all."

Margaret turned to her with a bemused expression and a little shake of her head. "Well, they do not know what they were missing then. And mark my words, Mother will like you very well indeed."

"Forgive me if I should not ask. If your mother was reluctant to send you to school, then why are you attending? Pray do not think I am unhappy with you, I was just wondering—"

"No, no, it is fine for you to ask. I quite understand. It was my brother who thought we should go for a term or two. He said my father wished to send us to finishing school, to make us into fine young ladies. It is not possible now, but Robert was determined to do what he could to honor Papa's wishes. He found Mrs. Goddard's school very acceptable and believed it would help us to feel ready to go out into society. For all that he is a crosspatch, he is a very good brother."

"That is very thoughtful of him. Does being introduced into society frighten you?"

"A little…no I cannot lie; it is more than a little. As much as I like meeting new people, somehow the idea of it leaves me all churny and knotted inside." Margaret pressed a hand to her belly. "And you?"

"I never thought about it much. Mrs. Goddard said I should be introduced though, and I feel just the same way."

"Oh, I am so glad it is not just me! It is another thing we must talk to Rachel about for she is just as anxious as I. Perhaps we might be able to do it together, at least some of it. I should feel so much better with you there with us. Perhaps Mama could suggest that you be included in invitations we receive. We would certainly include you in anything we would host, assuming Robert would permit us to host anything. He is not much for company in the evenings."

Harriet hesitated. "Perhaps—"

"No, it will be fine. He agreed to Mama's invitation so if he does not like it, that is his own fault. He will probably go hide in his office after dinner anyway, so we will see very little of him. Now enough of that. Tell me what you thought of the last chapter of *Romance of the Forest*."

Harriet paused as the first glimpse of the Abbey Mills farm house came into view. It was a lovely, three story house with cheery windows and a front covered in friendly vines that waved a beckoned to her. Even with the backdrop of heavy clouds, it seemed warm and welcoming.

"So you like the house?"

"Does it always smile at you like that when you approach?"

"Smile? I never thought of it that way, but I suppose it does. You will like it even more when you come inside." She pulled Harriet up the front path and in the door. "Mama! Mama! Look who I have brought."

Margaret took Harriet's bonnet and shawl and placed them on a small cabinet just beside the door.

The front door opened into a small hall with a room on either side. A stairway peeked out just beyond the left hand room, and a passage led to more rooms directly ahead. It was a little dark, but a warm, fuzzy kind of darkness, rather like a favorite wool blanket. Several chairs lined the hall bearing wraps and bonnets. A doll and toy horse lay on the floor nearby and a workbasket balanced on the edge of the bottom step.

Mrs. Goddard insisted the girls not leave their things outside their rooms and that their rooms be kept tidy and presentable at all times. This disarray was unfamiliar, but not in a displeasing way. It spoke of a liveliness and ease here, a place that was maintained for the comfort of those who lived there, not for the inspection of outsiders. Though Mrs. Goddard might censure the practice, it was really rather cozy and agreeable.

"Mama?"

"Here dear. I am here." A plump woman with grey-streaked hair peeking under her mobcap trundled into the hall. Her apron bore many smudges and she balanced a small girl of perhaps four years on her hip. The child cuddled close to her, laying her head on her mother's ample bosom, clearly and blissfully at peace. Exactly the right and proper expression for a child that age.

"See, Mama, I have brought Harriet to visit!"

"Shh, you will disturb your sister." Harriet pressed her fingers to her lips.

"She is right, Margaret." Mrs. Martin whispered. "I am pleased to make your acquaintance, Miss Smith." She bobbed in an inch-deep curtsey, probably all her knees could manage with the extra burden in her arms.

Harriet curtsied deep enough for both of them. "Thank you for inviting me, madam."

"Madam is it? Well there are some pretty manners, aren't there? We are pleased to have you even if my daughter failed to introduce us properly." She lifted an arched eyebrow at Margaret.

"Sorry, Mama." Margaret hung her head. "Mama, this is my friend, Harriet Smith. Harriet, this is my mother, Mrs. Martin."

"Much better. See you remember for the next time. Why do you think your brother is bearing the expense of sending you to school? Rachel is in the parlor. I am sure she will be pleased for your company. Go on now. I will call you for dinner after the little ones are fed." She shooed them toward the passage.

"Come this way." Margaret took her hand and guided her down the far passage to the parlor. "I had hoped she might allow us the drawing room on the occasion of your visit."

"I cannot imagine why. The drawing room is only for ladies and gentleman, and I am neither."

Margaret giggled.

They stepped into a largish room filled with the evidence of life and family. Chairs and tables, books, playthings, workbaskets, and a lap desk with a drawing half-done.

"What a wonderful room!" Harriet took two steps in and turned around to see everything.

"You cannot be serious. It is not nearly so fine—"

"It does not have to be fine to be—comfortable. That is what it is, comfortable and warm and friendly. How can you ever bear to leave it?"

"Quite easily." Rachel snorted from the smallish daybed near the fireplace. "When you have been asked to clean it often enough, one is very glad to take her leave."

"Oh, I did not see you there!" Harriet stopped her turn abruptly. She nearly stumbled over a small footstool.

Margaret caught her arm.

"I am glad you have come to see me." Rachel propped herself up on her elbows.

Harriet hurried to Rachel's side. "How is your ankle? Does it still pain you?"

"It is better now, I think, but still very sore to walk upon."

"I am very sorry to hear it. Mrs. Goddard permitted me to come on Margaret's insistence that I could cheer you up. So I consider that now my solemn charge. You must tell me how best to accomplish just that."

"Just seeing a friendly face is most cheering, I assure you. The little ones have been all a dither being kept inside all day. And Robert—oh, he has been an absolute ogre since he returned from town, grumping and stomping about that it should not rain on days he plans to be working on the fences."

"I am sure it is quite vexing to have one's plans foiled by ill weather. You must consider how much more difficult the weather can be when one must do their work outside." Harriet shrugged.

"Indeed it is."

She looked over her shoulder. Mr. Martin stood in the doorway, his muddy great coat dripping bits of dirt and clay on the floorboards. His round face resembled Mrs. Martin's too much for him to be any but her son.

"Robert! Do stop being so cross. Come in and be introduced to our friend, Miss Smith." Rachel said.

"I met her briefly this morning. Forgive me, I do not have time to socialize right now. I come bearing a message from mother. She asks if she may send Betsy,

James and Susan to you. Molly and Ann are a bit fussy at eating."

Margaret rolled her eyes and pouted. "Does she not remember we have a guest?"

Robert glowered.

"I am not at all bothered. I should very much enjoy their company." Harriet took half a step toward the door.

"But I hoped we could discuss the Romance of the Forest." Rachel folded her arms tightly across her chest.

"We will have plenty time to do that I am sure. I would like to meet your little brother and sisters."

Margaret huffed.

"I will tell mother." He dipped his head and disappeared.

"Now you have met Mr. Disagreeable," Rachel muttered.

"I am sure he is not so bad. He was not at all unpleasant this morning. "

"I am not sure I would agree. He was all but in high dudgeon by the time we reached Mrs. Goddard's this morning." Margaret flopped down at the end of the daybed.

"He is a good brother to us all, do not mistake that. But he works too hard and does not take the time for a spot of fun now and then."

"We should all be quite pleased—Mama included—if he would find some interest outside of the farm. If only he would read something other than farming magazines. Perhaps he could play cards or take up boxing."

"Oh that would be a sight!" Rachel sniggered. "Him in the boxing ring. With his temper, he would surely be champion in no time!"

Three young children dashed in and gathered around Harriet. Harriet knelt and opened her arms to them. "Now which of you is Susan?"

A little girl with a gap tooth smile waved.

"So you are Betsy and James?"

They nodded and drew closer.

"And do you like stories?"

"I do very much." Betsy nodded.

"Especially of knights and fairies," Susan added.

"Awww," James scuffed his foot and grumbled.

"What kind of stories do you like?" Harriet took his hand and met his gaze.

"Ones with dragons and ogres and swords." He crossed his arms over his chest. His scowl imitated his brother, but the frilled collar of his skeleton suit shirt softened the expression into something rather dear.

"So then it must be a story…" She turned to Betsy.

"A long one!"

"A long story about," she looked at Susan, "A knight and his fairy guardian." Susan clapped.

Harriet turned to James, "Who must find a magic sword to defeat an ogre to get to the dragon's lair and rescue—"

"A princess!" Becky cried.

"A princess from being eaten by the dragon."

Susan clapped and bounced. "Oh, that sounds like a wonderful story. Do tell us please!"

"Well then, come and sit close and I shall tell you." Harriet sat tailor style on the floor, her back against the daybed.

The children gathered around her, with Susan climbing into her lap.

"May we listen too?" Rachel asked, eyebrow raised.

"Not at all. I expect you to help me." She peeked over her shoulder at Margaret. "You as well."

"And how are we to do that when we do not know the tale you are telling?" Margaret peered down her nose.

"I am not a good storyteller." Rachel leaned back against her pillows and stared at the ceiling.

"You will be wonderful at it, you shall see. But for now, listen. Once upon a time…"

What a joy it was to have such a rapt audience for her little tale. Better yet, they were all so imaginative. They yelped and giggled at the sounds and voices provided by their sisters as the knight met his fairy guardian and prepared for his quest.

"Eh-hem." Mr. Martin cleared his throat in the doorway. "I fear I am intruding with most unwelcome news. Mother asked me to inform you that dinner is ready. The maid is to take the children to the nursery, and I am to help Rachel to the dining rom."

"No! No! That's not fair. We haven't finished our story yet." James stood and stomped his little booted foot.

"Do not take that attitude with me young man or you and I shall have a conversation in my study."

James covered his backside with both hands.

Margaret and Rachel coughed.

"Just a few more minutes, Robert, please." Betsy blinked up at him.

"No, no, you must do as your bother says. I will not have any unpleasantness on my account. After all, you would not want to make the good fairy sad, now, would you?" Harriet rose.

"No, but…" Susan pulled at her hand.

"I promise, I will tell you the rest of the story as soon as I am able. Perhaps if you are very good and quick to obey now, we might persuade your mother and good brother to allow you to come downstairs after dinner to hear the rest."

"Oh, please, Robert, may we?" The children rushed to him and grabbed his hands.

His eyes widened in something like panic. He glanced at Harriet.

Sometimes the older girls at school wore exactly the same expression. Poor man was quite over-whelmed at their attentions.

"He cannot say yes unless you are very good and do exactly as you are told." Harriet stepped toward them.

"Yes, Miss Smith." The girls curtsied, James bowed and they dashed upstairs, a bemused young maid following after them.

"I am sorry for any difficulty I may have caused with them. They are quite delightful." Harriet said.

Mr. Martin snorted. "I have heard them called may things, but delightful has rarely been among them. They seem quite well behaved for you."

Harriet shrugged. What was one to say to such a peculiar gaze and remark?

"Little ones always are. You should see her at school with the younger girls. They follow her like ducklings after a mama duck, all in a neat obedient little row." Rachel chuckled and reached toward her brother. "Help me up."

"Need I carry you?"

"No, I only need an arm to lean upon, I think." She took his hand and stood tentatively.

"Does it hurt very much?" Harriet asked.

"It is much better than this morning." She took an awkward step. "But I definitely need Robert's arm. Why do you two not go on? I will be slow, I fear. And do not rush me brother, with your grand big steps in those great boots of yours."

He muttered something. Probably best she could not discern what it was. His tone was quite disgruntled. Margaret took her arm and led her to the dining room.

༄Chapter 5

THE ROOM WAS JUST large enough to be comfortable and no larger. Exactly as she imagined a family dining room should be. Not stuffy and formal like those pictures in the Lady's Magazine—no this was a place where conversations might be had and stories told.

The table was laden with dishes of many good things—a few unfamiliar, but what was an unfamiliar dish among friends?

"Here," Margaret pointed to a chair. "You sit between Mama and I. Robert sits at the foot of the table where he might grump to his heart's content."

Why did she dwell so on her brother's ill humor? Truly he did not seem too bad.

Mrs. Martin shuffled in, bearing the final dish to the table.

"Roast pork? How very happy we are to see that tonight. It must be on account of your visit, Harriet." Rachel limped in on Robert's arm.

"I am pleased for your approval dear." Mrs. Martin clucked her tongue and sat down. "Now we have tench pie over there, stewed apples, broiled mushroom, stewed peas and lettuce, a bit of gravy, a lovely pudding and some pickles. Pass the platters and serve yourselves. We do not stand on ceremony or servants here."

"That is because we have none," Margaret whispered behind her hand.

"Are you complaining about servants again?" Robert grumbled under his breath as he carved the pork.

"We could use another girl in the house." Rachel passed a dish laden with peas and lettuce to her mother.

"And I could use more help in the barns and fields." He passed the platter of meat to Margaret. "But we neither can have what we want right now. It is better to be thankful for the help we can have than to spend too freely on what we do not strictly need."

"That is what you always say, 'we should not spend too freely' and we are forever—"

"Complaining about what you do not have instead of making do with what you do. I do not imagine Miss Smith is accustomed to many servants waiting on her needs hand and foot." His lip curled back in a peculiar way, not exactly a sneer, but probably not approving either.

"No, sir. Mrs. Goddard does not employ many servants at all. We are often needed to help with the work of the house."

"Oh, do not tell him that, he will want to dismiss our maid!" Rachel huffed.

Harriet stared at her plate and twisted the napkin in her hap. Her cheeks prickled and she swallowed hard. It was as Belinda had foretold, she would say something stupid and prove herself an utter cake.

"I would not dare do such a thing. The work of the house barely gets done as it is . We have as many hands working to undo the good work as those working to accomplish it."

Mrs. Martin sat up very straight and leaned forward on her elbows. "Robert, that is a fine thing to talk of over dinner when we are hosting a guest. Pray have some consideration for those whose feelings are perhaps a bit finer than your own."

Now Mrs. Martin was upset. Could this get any worse?

Robert exhaled heavily and leaned back in his chair. "In time, Providence willing, these things that you ask for may very well happen, albeit with some good planning and hard work. Did I not promise you—"

"Yes, you did and the gig is very fine, even if it is not new," Rachel said very softly, her color high.

"How splendid it must be to have your own transport and to be able to go from place to place whenever you wish." Harriet peeked up. "When one has no alternative but to walk, there are a great many things that one cannot do."

Mr. Martin's expression softened. "Thank you, Miss Smith. You see, your friend understands your good fortune quite well."

"You do not need to side with him you know." Rachel batted her eyes at her brother. "He can fuss all he likes, but you are our guest and you are safe from him."

"Perhaps you should consider what he is saying though. There is a great deal of good sense—"

Mr. Martin laughed heartily. "You see, it is as I have told you so often. Ask anyone of wit and practicality and they will find my judgments sound."

"She may find your decisions sound, but she has never lived with you when you are cross. If she had, she might not be so quick to agree with you." Margaret chuckled, eyes filled with warmth.

Harriet sighed a little and picked up her fork. Pray let there be no more disgruntled opinions.

Mrs. Martin turned toward Harriet. "So, Miss Smith, how did you keep the children so quiet after I sent them to you. I daresay, I only notice them so silent when they are into some new mischief. I do hope they did not trouble you."

"They are very dear children and no trouble at all."

All the Martins laughed.

"I daresay you are being overly generous for the sake of your hostess." Mrs. Martin winked. "I know my children well enough. I insist you share your secret though."

Harriet shrugged. "They like to hear stories, and I was happy to tell one."

"She is such a good storyteller, Mama," Rachel said.

"Indeed—she even bade us do voices for the characters. I was a fairy guardian." Margaret's pitch rose to match the fairy's "Who followed a brave knight on a quest."

"Your father used to tell you such tales when you were their age." Mrs. Martin smiled broadly.

"And he did such scary voices!" Margaret half-stood and clutched the edge of the table. "Do you remember when he told of the pirate and the sea monster?"

Rachel's eyes grew wide. "I do! Oh, his monster gave me shivers."

"Who dares cross into my territory—I did not bid these puny vessels of wood and cloth here." A deep gravel voice boomed.

"Robert!" Margaret and Rachel cried.

"You sound just like your father." Mrs. Martin's jaw dropped.

"That is a very good pirate." Harriet squeaked. And a very scary one. His sisters would probably argue that came very naturally to him.

He looked at her so oddly—what ever could it mean?

"Oh, oh! You might be the ogre and the dragon for our story!" Rachel said. "What do you think?"

"What a splendid idea!" Margaret nodded. "Mama, might we bring the children downstairs after dinner and finish our story? With Robert's help it will be so much better!"

He shook his head. "No, I do not think so. There is work in my office I should attend."

Harriet bit her lip. No, he was upset again. And it was her fault!

He looked away.

Was he angry… or perhaps just shy?

"You see, he is an ogre, always working and never enjoying anything." Margaret harrumphed.

The barest hint of a frown turned his lips down. Heavens! He was hurt by her accusation.

If he was shy, then her complaint was not fair at all. Even the shyest girls at Mrs. Goddard's were able to enjoy the parlor and have fun in the evenings when they felt comfortable and welcome enough.

"You should not speak to your brother so. I am sure your work is very important, Mr. Martin. It must be very impertinent of me to ask, but could you, would you spare a few minutes with us? I think it would mean a great deal to the children who must be missing their father's tales." She pressed her lips tight. Perhaps she had said too much and been very rude indeed.

Mr. Martin's face softened into something quite like little James', quite agreeable and dear. He seemed to think for quite a long moment. "I suppose you are right, Miss Smith. I can. I expect then I should also fetch some apples to roast on the fire as well?"

Margaret gasped.

"That is a fine idea. James is big enough for that duty if you would be willing to teach him. He should enjoy that very much indeed." Mrs. Martin stared wide-eyed at him.

Rachel leaned toward Harriet and whispered. "What an influence you have on our dear brother. I hardly know him right now."

Harriet pressed her hands to very hot cheeks. Oh, that they would not jest so. She would soon turn very red no doubt and they would all remark upon it. It was so hard to be a ginger sometimes.

"Do not tease your friend. Can you not see she does not like it?" Robert's voice was firm, almost sharp, and his gaze fixed upon her.

"I…it…pray do not…"

Rachel looked truly repentant and not a little startled. "Do forgive me. I meant nothing by it. How very thoughtless of me, especially when you have come out of your way to keep company with me."

"Pray do not worry, it is nothing, truly. Mrs. Goddard discourages her students from bantering with one another for fear of hard feelings. I am simply not accustomed to the teasing of brothers and sisters."

"You have none, Miss Smith?" he asked.

"No, sir. I…I have no family of my own." There, her secret was out, more gently that Belinda would have announced it, but still, there it was, open for all to see.

Mrs. Goddard had cautioned her to avoid talking about it for it would lead to unfavorable talk. Instead she should mention the annuity that would ensure her comfortable maintenance. That proved well enough she was cared for by someone.

While it was true, somehow it felt a bit duplicitous. That was far more uncomfortable than the truth. Besides, if the elder Martins were to be her friends, they would know the truth eventually, why delay the inevitable?

She peeked up at him.

"Perhaps then, you should spend more time among mine." His gaze returned to his plate.

Mrs. Martin's lips crooked in a peculiar half-smile. "Some more tench pie dear?" She handed Harriet a dish.

Margaret did moderate her teasing after her brother's reprimand and the remainder of the meal was most agreeable. Dinners at Mrs. Goddard's were certainly pleasant, but there was something different here, amidst a real home and family—a warmth, a belonging, a camaraderie unfamiliar, but compelling. Was this what Mrs. Goddard thought of when she said she wished for Harriet to have a home of her own?

Mrs. Martin excused herself to fetch the children whilst Harriet and the rest returned to the parlor.

Robert helped Rachel to the daybed and disappeared again, mumbling something about apples and toast.

"He truly is on his best behavior tonight, Harriet." Rachel settled a light blanket over her lap, a wistful look on her face. "It has been a very long time since I have seen him like this."

"Like what?"

"So agreeable. He can be so stand-offish when we have guests—especially young ladies. He barely says a word at the table and then disappears into his study after dinner to read. He rarely sits with us and never has the inclination to join in any kind of amusements."

Margaret glanced over her shoulder. "He really is a very good brother, but his manners of late have been most unpleasant. I cannot fathom why though. The farm is doing well, insofar as I am able to understand. He even said Mr. Knightly, who owns the land, is very impressed with his efforts. He is such a mystery to us all."

The children tumbled in. The older girls dragged the youngest two girls, Molly and Ann, directly to Harriet.

"They did not get to hear the beginning of the story." Susan folded her little arms over her chest and tried to muster a look as commanding as her brother's. The attempt was good, though on a miniature scale.

"They are sad for missing it," Betsy added a little shyly. Apparently she was like her eldest brother, too.

"I suppose there is only one thing for it—we must begin again. Come." She beckoned them near the fireplace and sat on the floor.

The littlest two settled on her lap, the others tucked in very close.

"Are you sure you want them all piled upon you like a heap of puppies?" Mrs. Martin cocked her head, a funny puzzled glint in her eyes.

"I am quite comfortable, thank you." Harriet looked down at the shining little faces in her arms. "Now then, shall we start at the beginning? Margaret and Rachel, you shall help me again?"

"And Robert, too!" Rachel pointed at the doorway where Robert stood, arms laden with a basket and a large pot.

"What do you have there?" Mrs. Martin took the basket.

"I thought some warm cider might be pleasant." He trundled past Harriet and the children and set up the pot on the hob. "Now James, it shall be your job to make us toast and roast apples."

The little boy jumped to his brother's side. "Truly?"

"You are big enough now. Watch carefully." Mr. Martin placed a plate for finished toast on a fire-cat near the fire and showed James how to set the bread up in a toasting fork. "Now, this is the part that requires the most skill."

James edged in very close. Mr. Martin produced a roll of string and a folding knife from his pocket. He measured out a length of twine and cut it. Nimble fingers tied a neat knot around the apple stem. He reached into the top center of the fireplace.

"You must tie the other end of the string around the nail just here. Take care you get it close enough to the fire to roast it properly, but not so close that you allow it to burn."

"I will be very careful!" James' eyes shone. Perhaps this new responsibility was even better than a story with ogres and dragons.

Mr. Martin pulled a stool close to the fire and sat near James. "Now how did the tale start, Miss Smith?" His mouth turned up at the corners just a bit, not a full smile, but his eyes made her insides feel all warm and fuzzy.

"Once in a land, far across the sea, behind the mountains and fed by a crystal river, there dwelled..."

How dear the children's faces appeared as they hung on every word of the tale. Even better though, were their delighted shrieks and giggles as even Mrs. Martin joined her eldest children in adding sounds and voices to the tale. None of them had ever heard their mother whistle like a bird before. She was remarkably good. Mr. Martin made for a credible ogre and an even more ferocious dragon. Perhaps a bit too much so. Little Ann might have nightmares from the fright it gave her.

Ogre and dragon vanquished and princess rescued, the story came to a close, but too many good feelings and high spirits abounded to end the evening. Margaret suggested a game of charades which was readily agreed upon as an excellent plan.

Harriet hung back a little. Mr. Martin offered her a roast apple, slightly overdone on one side.

"Thank you very kindly, sir."

"James is still learning." He peered at her. "Are you quite well?"

"I am fine, thank you."

"No, something bothers you. Pray, tell me."

Warm prickles crept up her neck. "It is only that I do not prefer charades, nothing more."

"It cannot be because you do not like to perform in company. Your storytelling was quite memorable."

"No, I just," she swallowed, "I fear I am quite stupid at guessing riddles and the like. I am always puzzled and confused." She dragged her foot along the carpet.

How was it this man managed to draw her two most uncomfortable secrets from her both in the same evening?

"I do not like it when I am made to feel stupid, either."

She looked up into very kind eyes. "I can hardly imagine you being stupid at anything. You must be very clever indeed to earn the praise of your landlord. I have heard tell that he is a very shrewd man."

"I am surprised you would have heard of him."

"Mrs. Goddard mentions him sometimes, always in words of praise at his kindness and generosity in the community. I should think it very telling a man like that would think well of you."

"You are too kind. My sisters are quick to remind me that my rather appalling lack of eloquence leaves me looking rather clownish. It seems I embarrass them by it." He glanced across the room.

"In my hearing, they have never described you as anything but an excellent brother." Perhaps that was a bit of a fudge, but close enough to a truth. They had certainly never called him clownish.

"Then I suppose those remarks are only for my hearing, perhaps in the hope of forcing some improvement in me. Sadly, it is quite a hopeless cause."

"As hopeless as me guessing at riddles? I hardly think so."

"Would you fancy a board game, perhaps?" He pointed with his chin to a small table with a game board set up on it. "It is rather silly, really, but my brother and sister find it quite amusing."

"I would like that, unless you think Rachel or Margaret—or your mother might be—"

"I am sure they will be very glad to see me play at anything. May I get you some cider?"

"Thank you."

He ladled out a cup and handed it to her as they walked to the game table.

Mr. Martin was quite correct, the game was quite silly. But that only provoked him to poke fun at it, revealing a wry wit. Margaret, with Rachel on her arm came to inspect their pastime and the sisters added their own droll observations on the entire scene. Had she ever laughed so much in a single evening? Mrs. Goddard cautioned her often against too much laughter—it was unladylike. But among such gay company who would not be prone to mirth?

"Robert, come help me," Mrs. Martin called in a hoarse whisper.

Molly and Anne curled against her sides, quite asleep. James sat on the floor against her knees, chin to his chest, snoring softly. "I don't want to wake them to put them to bed."

"I will carry James up. He is much too big for you." He lifted the boy to his shoulder.

"Margaret, help Susan and Betsy up."

"I can take Ann for you." Harriet reached for the sleeping girl.

"That is very kind." Mrs. Martin maneuvered Molly to her shoulder and followed Margaret and the other two youngsters upstairs.

The nursery was a snug cozy place with three little beds piled high with pillows and dolls and a stuffed dog. Other toys lined the walls and an off-kilter set of shelves. The rug was roughly braided of rags, probably clothes worn to ribbons through the years. What stories might it tell?

"Would you move Brownie aside so I can put James down?" Mr. Martin whispered.

Harriet picked up the toy and tucked it under the sleeping boy's arm.

Mr. Martin pointed to Ann's bed and Harriet laid down her charge.

"Go back down to Rachel. I will help Margaret with the other two, and we will be down shortly." Mrs. Martin tucked Molly under her blanket.

Harriet followed Mr. Martin out. He had broad shoulders and a trim figure. His coat was perhaps not as stylish as a true gentleman's, but his manners were altogether pleasing and gentlemanly. Belinda might not find him polished enough for her preferences, but Mrs. Goddard would like him very much. How could his sisters find him disagreeable?

He led her down the stairs, but paused half way. "Have you a taste for ginger?" He pulled a small tin from his pocket.

"Are those from Mr. Rose's shop?"

"Yes, I am quite convinced he makes the best ginger comfits."

"They are Mrs. Goddard's favorite as well. She has had them in the house for as long as I can remember. The other girls prefer the lavender ones, but I like the ginger best." She tugged a little curl beside her ear.

"Then please, have one." He took one and pressed the tin a little closer to her.

She giggled and popped one in her mouth.

"I confess I have a real fondness for ginger." He looked at her quite strangely.

What did that look mean? It felt vaguely as though he expected her to understand something, but whatever could he mean?

"Miss Smith, I fear this may be a shocking question but I am not at all good at proper and polite speeches. Have you enjoyed your evening with us?"

"I can hardly think of a pleasanter evening I have spent anywhere. Have I in some way offended you that you would think that of me?"

"You are comfortable in the midst of our modest and well lived-in home, surrounded by a large, unruly family?"

"I…I…I think it quite delightful and comfortable. One can tell a family lives and plays and laughs here. That must be a very good thing, must it not?" She tapped the carpet with her toes. "I have never liked too much tidiness in a place, though Mrs. Goddard does not agree."

He leaned a little closer, peering deep into her eyes, eyebrow lifted in a funny sort of question, but what was he asking?

My, his were such an alluring hazel-grey like heavy spring clouds over the fields. Not the thundery kind, but the ones that brought that drenching refreshing sort of rain that left everything feeling fresh and new.

"I am not accustomed to meeting new people. Your family, all of them, have made me feel ever so welcome and at ease. At Mrs. Goddard's, I help with the little girls and find them ever so dear. I am never as happy as I am with them. Now, really, I must ask, have I displeased or offended you in some way sir?

"Not at all, why do you say that?"

"You have asked so many questions and are staring at me with a most peculiar expression. I can only guess that it is because I have done something wrong. I have been afraid all night that perhaps you or your mother or your brother and sisters would not like me very much and might even regret that you invited me."

The corner of his lips came up and his cheek dimpled. "You were right, Miss Smith. You are quite hopeless at guessing things."

His eyes crinkled up at the sides. That must mean he was content, not offended. Hopefully it did.

"You have not at all been disagreeable, Miss Smith, not at all." He offered her his arm and they continued downstairs.

She had never taken a man's arm before. How strong he was, his arm so hard beneath her hand. He smelled of the farm and the earth and a touch of soap. Not at all like the old solicitor who sometimes visited Mrs. Goddard. No, Mr. Martin's scent was very...comfortable.

At the base of the stairs, he paused again. "Would you...that is to say...ah...did you find this evening pleasant?"

"I believe I just said so, but yes, I did."

"Enough that you would care to repeat the experience?"

"I know I should say that there are other girls at the school who would surely enjoy an invitation from your sisters and that it is very selfish of me to say so, but yes, it was all so lovely. I can hardly think of anything I would rather do."

He nodded sharply, an exhaled a short breath. "I shall speak to my mother then and recommend that she extend the invitation very soon."

"That is most kind of you, Mr. Martin. I think Margaret and Rachel will be pleased. Margaret feared you might not be a great lover of company on such an evening as this."

"In that, Miss Smith, she was very wrong." He pressed her fingers against his arm with his large calloused hand.

"Is that you Robert?" Rachel called from the parlor. "Oh, do not gad about so. It is very dull indeed all alone here.

"Shall we join her?" He gestured toward the parlor and pulled his arm in a little tighter and with it Harriet a mite closer.

"I think it a lovely idea."

So this was what a family home was like. Mrs. Goddard was right. This was exactly the sort of thing that would suit her very well indeed.

❧Chapter 6

Anniversary at Abbey Mills Farm

RAIN PELTED THE WINDOW even as the sun tried to rise. Warm beneath the soft quilt made by dearest Mrs. Martin to celebrate their wedding, Harriet cuddled into her husband's shoulder. "I suppose you shall not be able to mend fences today after all."

Robert Martin leaned against the headboard and muttered under his breath.

She stroked his face. "Do not get all grumbly and ogreish—you would not wish to prove your sisters correct."

"About what? That I am churlish and disagreeable when it rains?" He folded his arms over his chest.

"Indeed." She looked up into his face. All these days now and she still loved seeing the bleary-eyed look he always wore in the mornings.

"But I am exceedingly disagreeable in foul weather." He huffed as if to prove his point.

"I cannot agree." She rolled to her side and propped up on an elbow. "Was it not on a day very much like today, one on which you could not mend fences, that we first met?"

"Indeed it was." He drew her very close. "Have I told you how very thankful I am that we did?"

She kissed his cheek. "Once or twice I believe."

"Perhaps I should again." He turned toward her and laid his hand on her increasing belly. "How is little Robert George Martin today?"

"How can we say when we do not know that indeed our wee one is a Robert or... a little girl? What shall her name be if—"

"Anything but Emma." His voice turned cross as it always did when he referred to her.

"You have not yet forgiven her?"

"Forgiven, perhaps. After all, I no longer wish to do or say any one of a number of untoward things when I see her." He rubbed his palm with his thumb.

"But is that forgiveness, or your friendship for Mr. Knightly?"

"A touch of both I suppose. I still cannot understand why he would take such a silly woman as a wife."

Harriet plucked at the hem on the sheets. "She has improved."

"She has ceased her matching, I will grant you. But I still doubt her good sense."

"What use has someone of her station for good sense? She has servants, and a husband for that."

"Now Harriet, what kind of statement is that? You very well know how much I rely upon your good judgment, especially where my younger sisters and brother are concerned. Now you are free of her, I am entirely confident in your sagacity. The new Mrs. Knightly is an entirely different matter. She is clever and silly, a disastrous combination in a woman of wealth and breeding." He grumbled deep in his chest, the way he did when he was truly and deeply unhappy.

"Her interference was well meant."

"But insupportable. How many months of misery did she inflict upon all of us? You cannot tell me you were happy whilst she played with your hopes and affections."

"No." Harriet pulled away slightly. "I do not like to think of it at all. I feel very foolish and stupid whenever I think of it."

"I am sorry." He reached for her, but she scooted away. "No, do not do that. Come here." He sat up and pulled her very close against his chest. "I cannot bear the thought of you distancing yourself from me again."

"How can you be so kind to me after—"

"Dearest wife of mine." He laid his chin on top of her head and his arms around her belly. "Let us settle this once and for all. Yes, I am disappointed that you were influenced by Miss Woodhouse and Mrs. Goddard, but my true unhappiness in the matter is laid at their feet, not yours. And with respect to Mrs. Goddard, she has been a mother to you. It is a testament to your good heart and loving disposition that you should have listened to her and the friend she pushed you towards."

"I should not have been so flattered by her attentions that I allowed her whims to overrule my own judgment and inclinations. I am grateful Mr. Knightly had a better sense of Miss Woodhouse's shortcomings and kept your spirits up."

"Him I consider the truest of friends. Without him I would have lost hope." He kissed the top of her head. "Do you resent…that is are you unhappy that I have asked you not to call upon Mrs. Knightly?"

"No, not so much. I should want to visit her, but it is all awkwardness and politeness that is very tiresome when I do see her. I am just thankful you still encourage our connection with Mrs. Goddard."

"She is far easier to reconcile. Who would not pursue the best for their child?"

"You will be gratified to know, she is in full agreement with me. You are the best thing for me."

He kissed her deeply, satisfaction rumbling in the back of his throat. "Do not ever forget."

She turned her face up and rubbed her cheek on his, enjoying the scratch of his stubble. "You will be an excellent father, you know."

"I want to do well by you Harriet, both of you." He stroked her belly and the baby kicked under his hand.

"It seems your child thinks you will."

"As long as neither of you stop believing that, I will be a very happy man."

"I think then, you are in a very good way to be so."

Enjoy other books in the Series:
Snowbound at Hartfield
A Most Affectionate Mother
Inspiration

Acknowledgments

So many people have helped me along the journey taking this from an idea to a reality.

Abigail, Jan, Ruth, Anji, Debbie and Julie thank you so much for cold reading, proof reading and being honest!

And my dear friend Cathy, my biggest cheerleader, you have kept me from chickening out more than once! Thank you!

Other Books by Maria Grace

Sweet Tea Stories:
A Spot of Sweet Tea: Hopes and Beginnings
Snowbound at Hartfield
A Most Affectionate Mother
Inspiration

Darcy Family Christmas Series:
Darcy and Elizabeth: Christmas 1811
The Darcy's First Christmas
From Admiration to Love

Given Good Principles Series:
Darcy's Decision
The Future Mrs. Darcy
All the Appearance of Goodness
Twelfth Night at Longbourn

The Queen of Rosings Park Series:
Mistaking Her Character
The Trouble to Check Her
A Less Agreeable Man

Fine Eyes and Pert Opinions
Remember the Past
The Darcy Brothers

A Jane Austen Regency Life Series:
A Jane Austen Christmas: Regency Christmas Traditions
Courtship and Marriage in Jane Austen's World

How Jane Austen Kept her Cook: An A to Z History of Georgian Ice Cream

Jane Austen's Dragons Series:
A Proper Introduction to Dragons
Pemberley: Mr. Darcy's Dragon
Longbourn: Dragon Entail
Netherfield:Rogue Dragon
The Dragons of Kellynch
Kellynch Dragon Persuasion

Behind the Scenes Anthologies (with Austen Variations):
Pride and Prejudice: Behind the Scenes
Persuasion: Behind the Scenes

Non-fiction Anthologies
Castles, Customs, and Kings Vol. 1
Castles, Customs, and Kings Vol. 2
Putting the Science in Fiction

Available in paperback, e-book, and audiobook format.

On Line Exclusives at:

Bonus and deleted scenes
Regency Life Series

Free e-books:

Rising Waters: Hurricane Harvey Memoirs
Lady Catherine's Cat
A Gift from Rosings Park
Bits of Bobbin Lace
Half Agony, Half Hope: New Reflections on Persuasion
Four Days in April

About the Author

Six-time BRAG Medallion Honoree, #1 Best-selling Historical Fantasy author Maria Grace has her PhD in Educational Psychology and is a 16-year veteran of the university classroom where she taught courses in human growth and development, learning, test development and counseling. None of which have anything to do with her undergraduate studies in economics/sociology/managerial studies/behavior sciences. She pretends to be a mild-mannered writer/cat-lady, but most of her vacations require helmets and waivers or historical costumes, usually not at the same time.

She writes Gaslamp fantasy, historical romance and non-fiction to help justify her research addiction.

She can be contacted at:

author.MariaGrace@gmail.com

Facebook:
http://facebook.com/AuthorMariaGrace

On Amazon.com:
http://amazon.com/author/mariagrace

Random Bits of Fascination
(http://RandomBitsofFascination.com)

Austen Variations (http://AustenVariations.com)

English Historical Fiction Authors
(http://EnglshHistoryAuthors.blogspot.com)

White Soup Press (http://whitesouppress.com/)

On Twitter @WriteMariaGrace

On Pinterest: http://pinterest.com/mariagrace423/